THE PICKUP

Tracy Swanson was on the verge of hysteria.

She had awakened some minutes earlier—to the sound of wind shrieking across the flat top of the wooden box in which she was imprisoned—to find herself bound and gagged.

It all came rushing back to her: The kitten and the old truck and . . . the man, the horrible, smelly old man. She remembered him lifting her, his rotten breath worse than whatever he had sprayed into her face to knock her out. . . .

Tracy tried to pull her thoughts together. She was not unintelligent and it had already occurred to her that she was being kidnapped by the fat man. He must have been watching her, waiting for the right moment.

The truck lurched again and began slowing and a horrible thought crept into her mind. Suppose the fat man hadn't taken her for money at all. Ignoring the pain in her side, Tracy struggled with new energy to slip her hands free from the tight bonds encircling her wrists. A fine curtain of dust filtered into the box through the air holes.

Books by Michael O'Rourke

Darkling
The Bad Thing

Coming Soon:

The Undine

Available from HarperPaperbacks

The Bad Thing

MICHAEL
O'ROURKE

📚 HarperPaperbacks
A Division of HarperCollinsPublishers

This is a work of fiction. The characters, incidents, and dialogues are products of the author's imagination and are not to be construed as real. Any resemblance to actual events or persons, living or dead, is entirely coincidental.

HarperPaperbacks *A Division of* HarperCollins*Publishers*
10 East 53rd Street, New York, N.Y. 10022

Copyright © 1995 by Michael O'Rourke
All rights reserved. No part of this book may be used or reproduced in any manner whatsoever without written permission of the publisher, except in the case of brief quotations embodied in critical articles and reviews. For information address HarperCollins*Publishers*,
10 East 53rd Street, New York, N.Y. 10022.

Cover illustration by Mark Garro

First printing: March 1995

Printed in the United States of America

HarperPaperbacks and colophon are trademarks of HarperCollins*Publishers*

❖ 10 9 8 7 6 5 4 3 2 1

To Jon and Michelle Jones, for their encouragement, to Katie Tso, for her wisdom, and to Kelly Reno, for her faith, this book is affectionately dedicated.

We have done with Hope and Honor, we are lost
    to Love and Truth,
We are dropping down the ladder rung by rung;
And the measure of our torment is the measure
    of our youth.
God help us, for we knew the worst too young!

—Rudyard Kipling

He was outcast from life's feast.

—JAMES JOYCE

Prologue

SNOW.

Big fluffy clumps of the white stuff drifted into the public square, tufting the town Christmas tree with a fleecy mantle and transforming the harsh glare of the multicolored bulbs to a soft, fuzzy glow that seemed perfectly in tune with the carols being sung by the teenagers gathered on the tiered platform at its base.

Fifty feet away, at a parking space angled into the curb, Chris Kelly sat in his father's new Buick, watching the carolers and trying to pick Diana out of the crowd. A girl on the upper tier of the platform turned her face toward him and he recognized his cousin Shelly. That narrowed his choices considerably. Diana was Shelly's best friend and the two of them were never far apart.

Because Diana was nearly a head taller than Shelly, Chris lowered his gaze to the next tier and was rewarded with a glimpse of her long blond hair framed beneath the red muffler she had draped over her head. His heart skipped a beat and he glanced at the dashboard clock, impatient for the caroling to be over.

The Buick's engine purred softly beyond the warm cocoon of the luxurious interior and soft jets of air from the heater vents played against his face and knees. Chris flipped on the wipers, clearing a thin veil of snow from the windshield and affording himself a better view of Diana. She glanced his way and he grinned to himself, feeling in his pocket for the small gold box containing the sterling bracelet with both their names engraved above a pair of entwined hearts. He tried to imagine the look in her eyes when he gave it to her before the dance tonight.

There was a loud commotion on the street behind the Buick and he turned to see an old Ford convertible with blatting illegal mufflers threading its way through the light traffic on the square. A family of last-minute shoppers hurried across the snowy street to a car parked beside the Buick, and the Ford came to a halt. The driver gunned the engine impatiently while the family loaded their purchases into the trunk, then clambered into the car and backed out into the street. The space was hardly empty before the Ford screeched into it and slammed to a stop against the curb.

Chris grinned and rolled down his window as Sonny Lasco, a sharp-featured youth with an elaborate pompadour of shining black hair and a leather motorcycle jacket, got out of the Ford and began applying a strip of silvery duct tape to the patched convertible top.

"Hey, Lasco, isn't it a little late to be decorating for Christmas?" Chris called.

Sonny Lasco, whose propensity to fight at the drop of a hat had attained legendary proportions at Bremerton Central High, whirled and glared into the Buick's darkened interior.

"Who the fuck said that?" he yelled combatively.

Chris opened his door and stepped out into the snow. "Why, do you want to fight about it?"

"Kelly, you asshole, when did you get in?" Sonny's fighting face dissolved into a good-natured grin and he reached across the Ford's battered roof to clasp Chris's hand in a crushing grip.

"Couple of hours ago," said Chris, glancing at the roll of tape in the other's hand. "Don't tell me this junker's leaking again."

"Every time I turn the heater on it melts the snow on the top," griped Sonny. "Bastard lays a steady stream of icewater square in my crotch." He kicked the side of the Ford affectionately and produced a crumpled pack of Camels from a pocket of the leather jacket. He lit the cigarette with an old Zippo and blew out a thick cloud of smoke. "So how long you in for?"

Chris shrugged glumly. "Till New Year's. Then we pack up and move again."

"You lucky bastard," said Sonny. "Where to this time?"

"Hawaii," said Chris. He snatched the cigarette from Sonny's nicotine-stained fingers and helped himself to a long drag.

"Hawaii, no shit?" Sonny let out a low whistle and tilted his head in the direction of the carolers. "You told Diana yet?"

Chris shrugged. "I might not go," he said evasively. "I've been thinking about staying here with my grandfather and doing my senior year at Central High with you guys. . . ."

Sonny stared at him. "Are you nuts? You'd give up *Hawaii* to spend a year in this shithole? Man, you must have it really bad."

Chris grinned and passed the damp butt back to him. "Yeah, I guess I do."

Sonny evaluated the remains of the cigarette and tossed it into the snow. "Look, don't get me wrong, man, Diana's a great girl and all. But Hawaii? I'd give my left nut to go to Hawaii. Hell, to go anywhere. First damn thing I'm doing when I graduate—if I graduate—is joining the marines and getting out of this stinking place forever."

"Come on, Bremerton isn't that bad."

Sonny laughed bitterly. "That's easy for you to say. Your old man's this big hotshot army colonel who moves you to all these great places, and you only have to come back here for holidays and stuff."

"All those great places aren't that great," said Chris. "Believe me. Besides, I've been coming up here almost every weekend since we moved to Philadelphia last year. I've got friends here. . . ." He looked toward the carolers, who were starting in on a spirited rendition of "Jingle Bells," a sure sign that the program was drawing to a close. Diana's red scarf had slipped down onto her shoulders and snowflakes were collecting in her golden hair. She looked like an angel in the glow of the colored lights.

"And I've got Diana."

Sonny rolled his eyes and pulled his jacket up around his neck. "Hey, let's get into your car," he suggested. "I'm freezing my balls off."

Chris opened the driver's door and ducked gratefully into the warmth of the Buick. Sonny ran around to the other side and scrambled in beside him, rubbing his hands briskly over the heater vents. "Hey, nice car. Bet it set your old man back a bundle. I wish *my* heater worked this good. It's colder'n a witch's tit out there tonight!"

"Lasco, I'm curious about something," said Chris. "Do you talk that way around Shelly?"

"Shit, no." He grinned. "When it comes to the ladies, I'm a regular fucking gentleman."

A dozen spaces down from the Buick—and thirty feet closer to the carolers—another vehicle sat beneath the shadow of an overhanging elm tree. The interior lights of the old Chevy pickup truck had been disconnected so that nothing of the driver was visible from the outside except the occasional orange glow from the tip of his filtered cigarette.

His name was Johnny.

Johnny liked the girls.

Both liked them and hated them.

He spent hours watching them, observing how they walked and sat and tossed their heads. Their gestures and movements were a constant source of amazement to him: the way their smooth breasts and legs and buttocks moved beneath their clothing, the silken rustle of slips and panties when they walked near him, the *smell* of them; some smelled like candy and flowers, others like moonlight and the night.

Johnny dreamed constantly about the girls, lay in his narrow bunk at night thinking about doing things to them, dark, forbidden things that he knew in his heart were mortal sins.

Sins you burned in hell for.

That was how Johnny had come to hate them. For when he thought of the things he wanted to do to the girls, bad things—evil things—happened to him, things that sometimes made him forget who he was and that left the awful, embarrassing stains on his sheets and, sometimes even, in his underpants.

Johnny hated the girls because they were bad and because they made the sinful things happen to him, things he could not help. Still, he could not seem to stay away from the girls either, deliberately seeking them out—just to watch and fantasize about them from a distance—whenever he knew they would be around.

Times like this—Christmas Eve, when he felt alone and cold, like maybe he was the loneliest person in the world—were the worst.

Johnny looked at the glowing Christmas tree in the square and all the prettily dressed girls standing on the platform, their soft red mouths opening and closing beneath the colored lights, and he felt the bad thing beginning to happen beneath his overalls. He closed his eyes and prayed he could have one of the girls all to himself for just a little while. Then maybe he could make the bad thing stop happening.

The tall blond girl with the red scarf was the prettiest of them all. He had seen her before at the high school football games and knew by heart what her legs looked like, long and slender and tantalizing beneath the brief red cheerleader skirt she had worn.

Johnny had dreamed of that one many, many times. And always when he dreamed, the bad thing happened. The thing his mother had first cursed and beaten him for the night she had walked into the bathroom and found him in the tub looking at it when he was nine years old.

A slow, tortured frown crossed his flushed, porcine features as he relived the pain of what his mother had done to him that night, tying a loop of her thick black sewing thread around his tiny thing so that it would never, ever be bad again . . . repeating the hated ritual again and again for years afterward, until she had been certain he was cured.

But Johnny had not been cured. Not then. Not ever. He had carried the dark secret with him until his mother's dying day, terrified that she would find out and do something far worse to him.

After she had died he had tried using the thread himself . . . but it didn't work even as well as when she had done it, and he had finally stopped altogether. And then the bad thing had started happening all the time . . . and he thought about the girls more and more.

Johnny knew that one day—one day very soon—he would have to take one of the girls and make her pay for what they were all doing to him or he would surely go to hell as his mother had warned.

He looked up and realized that the singing had stopped. The girls were coming down off the platform, laughing and giggling and running through the snow. He watched the tall blond girl pass in front of the pickup truck. She glanced directly at the snow-encrusted windshield and he imagined that her eyes were burning straight into him, her evil gaze probing deep down into his overalls, making the bad thing happen. The thing that would one day condemn him to the everlasting agony and torment of Satan's fiery inferno.

She turned away and he watched as she hurried to a shiny new Buick parked a short distance away. A boy in black leather got out of the car and the girl got in to take his place beside the driver.

"Hi!" Diana slid into the front seat of the Buick and pressed her cold cheek against Chris's.

"Hi, yourself." He turned his head and their lips met in a long, delicious kiss, his tongue probing delicately for hers, tasting the peppermint on her breath.

"Okay, knock it off, you two, or you're going to get arrested for lewd conduct in a public place." They turned to look at Shelly, who had thrust her head into the car. She pulled off one of her knitted gloves and ran her hand across the silvery leather of the seat back. "Oh, my God," she murmured, "I could die for a car like this. Can we ride with you guys tonight? Please?"

"Hey, babe," said Sonny, coming up behind her and grabbing her around the waist while slipping a furtive hand beneath her bulky ski sweater, "can't you see they want to be alone?"

"*You* want to be alone, you mean." Shelly slapped his hands away and brushed a strand of loose red hair from her freckled forehead. She looked back at Chris and Diana and wrinkled her nose. "He's *such* an animal," she snarled.

"And she loves it," said Sonny, grabbing her in a bear hug and nuzzling beneath the collar of her turtleneck to plant a loud, smacking kiss on her neck.

"Yeah, well if you don't get a car with a decent heater pretty soon, pal, I'm going to die of pneumonia," Shelly groused. "Can you believe he actually wanted to go parking up on Roundtop last night?" she asked the other couple. "I checked the temperature. It was five degrees below zero. My goose bumps had goose bumps."

"Hey, I always warm you up, don't I?" Sonny asked.

Shelly rolled her eyes, pretending to ignore him. "You two going to the dance?" she asked.

Chris nodded. "That's what I came here for," he said. Diana poked him in the ribs and he sighed. "Hey, Shel, if you and the animal want to ride with us, it's okay."

Shelly wriggled free of Sonny's grasp and shook her head. "Thanks," she said. "He'd just pout all night if he had to ride in the backseat." She smiled and linked her arm with Sonny's. "Besides, for once he's probably right. You two do need to be alone. We'll see you at the dance."

"Don't do anything we wouldn't," yelled Sonny. He opened the door of the old Ford for Shelly, then slid in beside her. The powerful engine roared to life and the old car drove away.

"Well," said Diana, when they had gone.

Chris smiled. "I missed you."

"Me, too."

He pulled her to him and they shared a long, breathless kiss. "God, I really did miss you," he said.

She pressed her body closer to his, letting her plaid coat fall open and he placed a gentle hand on the firm swell of her breast. She sighed and placed her hand over his and they kissed again.

"I wish we could be together all the time," she whispered.

"Maybe we can." He nuzzled her ear. "I'm thinking about transferring to Central."

Diana pulled away and looked at him, her green eyes widening. "Oh, Chris, are you really?"

He nodded. "My folks are moving to Hawaii. I've just about convinced my dad that I'll have a better chance of getting into a good Ivy League school if I stick around this part of the country for interviews."

"You'd give up Hawaii to stay here . . . with me?"

Chris smiled. "Well, I don't really like pineapple all that much anyway."

Diana threw her arms around his neck. There were tears rolling down her cheeks. "Oh, darling, I love you. I really do. You won't be sorry. I swear to God."

"Hey, hey, hey!" He pulled away and dabbed at her cheeks with the end of the red scarf. "Hawaii wouldn't be any fun without my girl. Tell you what. We'll see it together on our honeymoon."

Diana fumbled in her pocket for a tissue and a small compact and examined her face in the mirror. "Oh, hell, look at me. My eyes are all red now."

Chris played with the radio while she dabbed powder on her nose. He found a Scranton station and the sweet, melodic sounds of the Beatles singing "I'll Follow the Sun" filled the car like a shining omen.

Diana turned to him and planted a tiny kiss on

his cheek. "I guess we'd better get to the dance," she whispered.

"In a minute." He pressed the small gold box into her hand. "Merry Christmas, honey."

She opened the box and gazed down at the silver bracelet. The entwined hearts with their initials carved into them gleamed in the dim light. "Oh, it's beautiful," she breathed. She slipped it onto her wrist and held it up to the windshield. "I'll never take it off."

"Next year it'll be a ring," he whispered.

They kissed again.

Johnny sat in the cab of the pickup watching the couple embracing in the car. The square had emptied with the end of the caroling and the two vehicles were the only ones remaining on the street.

He didn't know exactly what was going on in the other car—for though he was five years older than Chris Kelly, Johnny had never actually been alone with a girl—but his troubled mind filled in the details. The girl—*his girl*—was locked in an illicit embrace with the stranger in the shiny new Buick, her silken legs curled beneath her on the richly upholstered seat, her soft red mouth open to his. He squeezed his eyes shut and saw her hand traveling down to the other's waist, slim white fingers fumbling to undo his trousers, working, probing, touching. . . .

Johnny moaned in agony, fumbling for the buttons of his overalls. Struggling to stop the bad thing before it happened. Thick, calloused fingers grasped for the unruly member, squeezing, willing it to stop.

Too late.

He cried out, feeling the sticky wetness flooding his gray woolen drawers.

The girl. It was her fault. The very evilness of her—for making him do such a bad thing, for driving him one step closer to hell—nauseated and terrified him. He looked up, staring wide-eyed through the steamy window, certain that he would see the demon fire glowing in her eyes.

Two coal-bright spots of crimson glared back at him through the misty glass. He shrieked and cowered in his seat, certain that his destruction was at hand, that he was about to pay for all the bad things, just like his stern mother had promised each time she had wound the stout black thread about him.

Hellfire and eternal suffering would be his.

He waited.

The gleaming spots of ruby light grew suddenly brighter, sparkling through the crusted snow on the pane. A clot of mucus dribbled from Johnny's nose and he clasped his hands over his closely shaven head.

Nothing could save him.

The fiery spots of red light dimmed, then receded slowly into the mist, and he dared to breathe again. He crept to the window, cranked it down on rusting runners just in time to see the twin taillights of the Buick disappear around a corner half a block away. Brake lights! That was all it had been, brake lights.

His breath coming in harsh, sobbing gasps, Johnny clambered across the torn plastic seat, positioned himself behind the pickup's cracked steering wheel, and turned the ignition key. The tired battery ground the old starter motor noisily, its flat, monotonous whine echoing across the empty square. The engine finally caught, sputtering to life with a shudder that rocked the cancerous body of the truck on its squeaking springs.

His fevered mind racing, Johnny jammed the balky shift lever into reverse and the truck lurched out onto the street, its nearly bald tires spinning against the accumulation of fresh snow on the frozen pavement.

Slamming the shifter into first with a tortured clashing of gears, he started the truck rolling in the direction the Buick had taken, following the fresh, black tracks gleaming up from the snow-covered pavement.

He did not know exactly where he was going, but it seemed imperative not to let the evil girl in the Buick escape. The old truck rattled to the corner of the square past the glowing Christmas tree and he looked out at it through the open window, noticing for the first time the brilliant star shining at its very top: the golden star that was exactly like the one his mother had kept wrapped in wrinkled tissue in the cardboard whatnot box beneath her bed.

Each Christmas until she died, Johnny's

mother had carefully unwrapped the star, standing on a rickety kitchen chair in her rustling black skirts and placing it atop the scraggly discount tree that was the only kind they could ever afford.

The star was a symbol of goodness, pointing the way to heaven. That was what Johnny's mother had always told him, forbidding the addition of any other adornment or decoration to the naked tree. All below was blasphemous and evil, but the star was pure and untouched.

Johnny stared unblinking into the shining light. He realized with sudden clarity that his mother had been right. After all, hadn't he watched with his own eyes as the girl and the stranger had done the evil thing in the parked car beneath the holy star?

He knew exactly what he must do to end the torture the evil girl had inflicted upon him and save himself from the everlasting hellfire.

He would do it tonight.

Johnny's thin lips twisted into a satisfied smile and he imagined his mother's severe face beaming down on him from heaven.

He would show her.

She would see that he was a good boy after all.

The pretty blond girl would be his Christmas present to her.

BOOK ONE

A Lifetaker and a Heartbreaker

The Killer

JOHANNESBURG, SOUTH AFRICA
JULY 1994

C H R I S Kelly killed people.

He had been killing people for more than half of his adult life.

It was what he did.

Not the only thing he did, but the thing he did best.

Traveling primarily—but not always—to those distant and exotic parts of the world whose principal exports are disease and misery and injustice, on behalf of an obscure governmental subcontractor, he had made a career of dispatching various and sundry of his fellow humans to their respective Valhallahs.

Quietly, cleanly, efficiently.

His expertise as a killer had brought him to

Johannesburg on this pleasant winter afternoon. As he arrived on the Swissair flight from Zurich by way of Nairobi it occurred to him that he was a living anachronism. Being a professional assassin these days was something akin to pursuing a career as a White Hunter in an Africa long since given over to camera safaris.

Nobody did it anymore—with the possible exception of Israel, and maybe the Mafia.

Oh, there was still plenty of killing around, as a look at any morning newspaper would readily confirm. But, by and large, the game had long since been taken over by gifted amateurs. The career assassin was as out of date as Neanderthal man and the fountain pen.

For one thing, governments—always the largest employers of such specialists—had recently discovered that it was no longer politically correct to keep trained killers on their payrolls.

The fact that he was obsolete didn't trouble Chris Kelly in the least. He was growing tired of killing and now he dreamed of retiring with the substantial nest egg he'd accumulated over the past twenty-odd years.

Passing through immigration and customs at Jan Smuts Airport, South Africa's central arrival point for all international flights, was no more—or less—daunting than usual, despite the highly touted reforms of recent years.

The same smiling immigration clerks still stood behind their bright Formica counters, politely enquiring about the plans of new arrivals to the RSA, hyping the numerous private game reserves, the splendid wine country and the luxurious rail journeys to the Cape: They still handed out the colorful brochures reminding visitors of the fact that South Africa remained the continent's final bastion of strictly enforced wildlife conservation.

But as the fresh-scrubbed clerks, whose numbers now included a few black faces, chatted and examined visas, members of the infamous security police, anonymous men in identical plainclothes suits the dull, leaden color of gathering storm clouds, circled the arrivals lounge like vultures, eavesdropping on a conversation here, examining a passport there, opening heavy doors fitted with electronic locks and panels of one-way glass to confer in whispered tones with others of their kind.

Once, years earlier, Chris had attracted the attention of the dreaded SPs at Jan Smuts—he never discovered why—and was afforded a visit to the notorious Jo'burg Hilton, a strange Orwellian section of the modern concrete terminal fitted out with all the familiar pastel acoutrements common to Holiday Inns worldwide.

The Jo'burg Hilton was like a hotel in every respect. Bellmen carried your luggage to your standard Holiday Inn room, the latest model Sony color television broadcast CNN and SABC programs from a wood-colored Formica dresser and surprisingly good meals were served three times daily by polite, white-jacketed room service waiters.

The glasses in the bathrooms were even wrapped in crackly paper and a sanitary strip advised that your toilet had been freshly disinfected.

After that, however, the similarities abruptly ended.

In the Jo'burg Hilton, you see, the drapes at the far end of your spacious room—the end where you would normally expect to find a picture window overlooking the vast sweep of Johannesburg's famed Gold Reef—parted to reveal only a blank concrete wall. You might have noticed then that there was no telephone on the bedside table and, most disturbing of all, no knob on the inside of the door.

Guests of the Jo'burg Hilton remained in their rooms at the pleasure of the management until it was decided whether or not they posed a threat to state security. In the Republic of South Africa a threat to state security could have been a copy of *Newsweek* magazine—which had been declared a subversive publication—discovered in one's luggage.

On that previous visit to Johannesburg, Chris was unaccountably held for three days, then just as unaccountably released to go about his business. No explanation, or apology, was ever offered for his detention.

Fortunately, on this trip the men in gray expressed no interest whatsoever in the tall, middle-aged American in the rumpled JCPenney suit. He wondered if it mattered that the name on his passport was different from what it had been on his earlier visit.

Although he was ostensibly in the country this time to confer with several local artists about performing in an international music festival to be held in London the following spring, the apple-cheeked clerk gave him an enthusiastic pitch on a new elephant sanctuary, stamped his passport with a red seal, and sent him on his way to the rental car stand with a handful of brochures depicting the pleasures of auto caravaning along the Wild Coast.

After collecting his luggage and passing through the glass doors into the main lobby, he reset his old stainless steel Rolex to the local time and ducked into a gift shop on the busy concourse for a cup of bitter coffee, allowing the line at the car rental booth to diminish somewhat in length while he took his bearings.

"Black or white, sir?" The smiling coloured waitress behind the counter posed the standard question, to which he had always been tempted to specify that he would prefer his coffee good.

"White," he muttered, knowing that good was not an available option.

The waitress hurried off to get the thick, black coffee and the pot of steaming milk that, mixed together in equal amounts, would compose "white," and he unfolded the tourist map on the imitation marble countertop, locating his objective to the north of the city in the Transvaal and mentally converting kilometers to miles for a rough estimate of how long it would take to cover the distance by car.

Figuring into his calculations the fact that the

first two thirds of the trip would be covered on a no-speed-limit ultramodern interstate-type highway as good as any to be found in the States, and the remainder on dirt roads, he estimated he could do it in two hours.

The final part of the journey would be undertaken in the early morning hours of the next day along roads that a legend on the map warned were subject to the vagaries of terrorist mines, wandering cattle and, occasionally, marauding lions.

A land of startling contrasts, is Africa.

He sat back to study the route to his objective and tried to enjoy the coffee. He really didn't have to hurry now.

There was no one to kill until tomorrow morning.

Johnny

J O H N N Y had killed another man.

He hadn't meant or wanted to do it, but it had happened all the same and now he was frightened.

Other men had come to the woods in search of the one he had killed, men with guns and dogs and helicopters. Johnny had huddled in his secret place for days, listening in terror as the searchers had swarmed through the gullies and thickets, sometimes passing so close to his lair that he could hear them talking, smell the smoke from their cigarettes.

He was afraid that they would find the man and see that someone had killed him by smashing his head with a jagged rock, spilling his brains out onto the flat, mossy stones by the water where he had been fishing. The searchers would know then that the man had not simply become lost in the forest and met with an accident as sometimes happened. Johnny had seen that on TV.

If they found the man's body they would begin searching harder and detectives would come with flashing lights on their cars. He had seen that on TV, too. The detectives would take fingerprints and put pieces of the man's brain under their microscopes. And they would know that Johnny had done it. They would put him in handcuffs and aim guns at his head and call him names and hit him hard until he confessed. Then they would take him to court and a judge would send him to the slammer, a dark, frightening place where black weight lifters would cut him with knives made from spoons they had stolen from the kitchens. . . .

Johnny had buried his shaved head in his fat arms and hidden beneath his mother's stained and faded quilt, weeping bitterly at the progression of horrible possibilities marching relentlessly through his mind. He had tried everything he knew to make the awful thoughts go away, but still they came, each worse than the last.

The very worst one, the thing that frightened him the most about going to the slammer, was not the black weight lifters or the sharpened spoons or the brutal guards who would hit him with their billy clubs and call him names. People had always done bad things to Johnny, beating him up in school, and later, when he was all grown-up, calling him names and laughing at his baggy overalls and halting speech. He was used to such things. What worried Johnny more than all of that was what would happen to all of the girls.

The girls—Johnny's girls—needed him.

There was no one else in the whole world to take care of them. No one else even knew where they were.

No one would ever know.

Johnny was far too smart for that.

The searchers had stayed in the woods for many days, the roaring engines of their jeeps and motorcycles and the baying of their dogs shattering the still, peaceful air and frightening away the squirrels and bunnies and other small creatures that were Johnny's only friends.

On the third day, the men moved to another part of the mountain, a place far from Johnny's hiding place and even farther from the place where he had hidden the man's body, and he began to think they might not find it after all.

On the sixth day, after a flurry of early morning activity, during which a clattering helicopter had flown repeatedly over Johnny's hiding place, they had gone away.

He had waited until well after dark, finally peering cautiously out through the leafy screen of scrub oak at the entrance to his den. After a life spent dodging the cruel slings and arrows of a cold and unforgiving world he had developed a ferretlike cunning that was largely responsible for the fact that his activities in and around the forest had passed unnoticed for so long. Long after the sounds of the searchers had passed away, he remained half convinced that they might be trying to trick him into coming out into the open so they could jump him from behind the trees and take him to the slammer.

A small noise disturbed the underbrush below a shadowy copse of firs near him and he froze, waiting for the bright cop lights to flash in his eyes. Instead, a fat red squirrel with an enormous bushy tail scampered out into the moonlit clearing. Pausing to snatch a fallen nut from the soft carpet of leaves, the saucy creature had jammed it into its cheek and, noticing Johnny, sat up on its chubby little hind end and chattered an angry warning that had made him laugh out loud.

After that, he knew the searchers had really gone, although from time to time he still heard the sound of a motor or a distant voice and suspected that a few members of the man's family might still be looking for him. He had seen them early in the search, before the others had arrived, and was not worried. There was no chance that they would ever find the body.

Feeling very relieved, he stepped from his shelter and, after carefully concealing the opening from view, walked briskly down the narrow deer trail toward the distant road leading to the shed where he kept his truck. He was very hungry, having subsisted entirely on canned soup and orange soda for several days, and he whistled a merry little tune as he walked along through the dark forest, thinking of the massive dinner he planned to consume.

Later, after he had had his fill of fried chicken and gravy-soaked biscuits, he would go to see the girls. He bet they'd been missing him terribly, probably been scared without him. A smile creased his fat features. He would have to do something to make it up to them. Maybe he'd bring them all a special treat for being good girls and waiting patiently for his return.

They all loved Twinkies.

CHAPTER 3

An Honest Killer

KILLING people in the officially sanctioned pursuit of fixed political objectives was no longer the growth industry it had been in the heyday of the all-powerful clandestine agencies. Back then, in the hysteria-driven climate of the fifties and early sixties, everyone was literally blowing away everyone else on a regular basis, and any government worthy of a permanent seat on the U.N. Security Council had dozens of professionals on staff or, at the very least, on call.

Professional assassins had been a curious status symbol among governments and government agencies in those days, the very fact of their employment serving as a crude barometer of the importance of the secrets they allegedly protected, the desirability of the policies they promoted. So numerous did the killers become that at one time most existed in a chronic state of underemployment, a condition that had ultimately resulted in their respective employers expending most of their considerable budgets simply tracking down and eliminating one another's hired assassins.

Kelly had never been one of those civil service killers, although the romantic image of Champagne-sipping agency darlings with unlimited expense accounts and dark Ivy League suits were mostly the product of novelists' imaginations anyway. Those who actually survived the cold war were of the old school, and most had long since retired to write their memoirs or been posted to obscure diplomatic posts in third-world countries.

Chris Kelly came by his killing honestly.

Drafted into the marines as a brooding nineteen-year-old college dropout, so naturally had he taken to the M14 automatic rifle then being issued to marine infantrymen—an awesomely accurate device still thought by many experts to be the most precise combat weapon ever placed in the hands of the average American fighting man—that he bested several long-standing range records during the painful course of his recruit training at Parris Island, South Carolina.

Upon graduation from boot camp his exceptional knack for individual marksmanship had resulted in a somewhat unusual—and, he later discovered, highly sought after—posting to an elite marine reconnaissance unit and, eventually, an assignment as a sniper.

Following several additional months of specialized training in the arts of war, he was sent forth to ply his deadly trade in the cool, empty highlands of the former Republic of Vietnam, setting up his highly modified rifle on postcard-pretty hilltops to read tattered paperbacks and await—sometimes for days on end—the appearance of enemy soldiers in the misty valleys below his position; a lone assassin shooting moving targets from distances as great as half a mile away with the cool detachment of a mechanic performing the exacting task of lining up and replacing the torque bolts in the transmission of your daddy's old Chevy.

In the first months of those long, waiting days Diana's voice and face had come to him often; the remembered sounds of her sweet sighs, the way her soft breast had felt beneath his caress.

Her memory haunted him.

And along with the memories had come tears, and guilt. Had there been something he could have done that snowy night back in Bremerton? Someone he should have seen prowling about in the shadows behind the high school gym? Some subtle clue or warning he had overlooked?

He did not know.

That was the maddening part of the whole terrible nightmare.

Nobody knew what had become of Diana Casey.

His tears had faded with time; but not the memories—never the memories. Only the tears. Diana had settled down to a sweet, dull ache that was never far from his heart and Chris Kelly concentrated all his energies on his job.

Killing two or three or four faceless little black-clad figures who had had the singular misfortune to step into the crosshairs of his precisely aligned telescopic sights right after breakfast on what would have otherwise been perfectly nice days, he saw himself as a competent technician.

Nothing more.

To Chris, on those misty Vietnamese mornings, the killing was thoroughly dispassionate, a job that involved humanely dispatching each target that fell under his sights with a single well-placed shot to the head and then escaping silently along a prearranged route long before the victim's companions—if any remained alive—had crept out from behind whatever hasty cover they'd managed to find when he'd started shooting, to confirm that Comrade Charlie was indeed stone cold dead.

Much of his ability to rationalize what he did came with the certain knowledge that, had he been caught, it would surely have cost him his own life, probably in a manner so excruciating and horrible he would have welcomed the end when it came. It was an understandable exchange, and one that seemed to him at the time to be both fair and sporting. In later years he understood that he had been crazy then, that at some level, being caught and tortured to death by his adversaries was precisely what he had wanted.

Not because he felt anything any longer, but simply because he did not wish to go on living in a world so befouled and evil that an innocent girl could be snatched from the bosom of her friends and loved ones without a single trace remaining to prove that she had ever even existed.

Chris Kelly never regretted a single one of the faceless people he killed while he was in Vietnam, never even dreamed or thought about them. His country was at war and he was doing his job. If he himself was killed in the process, then so be it.

It probably helped that he no longer held any religious or spiritual beliefs of any kind.

After Diana had been taken from him there was nothing left to believe in anyway.

Except maybe evil.

The trip north to Warmbad—Vormbaad in the local Afrikaner dialect—was completely uneventful, as he had anticipated.

He pulled the rented South African-manufactured BMW off the motorway just before dusk and stopped to register at a guest house near the renowned natural hot springs, deposited his luggage in the pleasant room that had been reserved for him some days earlier, and changed into lightweight khakis and a woolen sport shirt and jacket, for July was the dead of winter in the Southern Hemisphere and there was a nip in the air.

With nothing to do for the next ten hours but wait, he strolled along the pleasant, tree-lined avenue that constituted the little resort town's main thoroughfare, examining the menus posted before the numerous cafés and restaurants, and briefly considering one of the highly touted mud baths.

The sulfurous smell at the door of the first bathhouse he looked into dissuaded him from proceeding any farther, and he retraced his steps to a homey-looking Greek restaurant where he was comfortably settled at a window table with a bottle of the excellent local Reisling and an attractive menu that was refreshingly devoid of the usual tourist fare of ostrich and springbok with monkey gland sauce.

He sampled the wine, ordered his meal, and watched the parade of elderly white strollers on the avenue while mentally reviewing the essential data that had been provided on his target for the following morning.

Muktar Saleem, age unknown, nationality Moroccan, was undisputedly the largest broker of contraband ivory and rhinoceros horn on the African continent. Masterminding a complex triangle that exchanged illegal animal products for Asian heroin, and that for black-market South African armaments that were ultimately sold for cash to half a dozen repressive dictatorships and terrorist organizations scattered about the Southern Hemisphere, Saleem had a reputation for complete and total brutality in his dealings—which included murders by flaying alive, disembowelment and, in at least one documented case, impalement of enemies and associates alike.

In short, nobody crossed Muktar Saleem, whose victims included the agents of at least three governments, as well as a high court official in his native Casablanca.

After nearly three years, Interpol was still at a complete loss to explain Saleem's rapid rise from obscurity.

Beginning as a minor supplier of light-skinned children of both sexes to the flesh peddlers of certain Middle Eastern capitals—an enterprise he was still reputed to maintain as a sop to his own twisted sexual preferences—Saleem had risen almost overnight to a position of international power unparalleled in criminal annals since the time of the Borgias.

Among the wilder theories that had sprung up in the criminal underworld to explain the Arab's sudden and unprecedented success was the widespread belief that he possessed Satanic powers.

Satanic powers or no, Muktar Saleem was clearly a man who badly needed killing.

Kelly anticipated no difficulty whatsoever in recognizing his target in the dim predawn light of the rural compound where he was scheduled to meet with a South African arms dealer. Although there were no known photographs of Saleem, it was widely known that he was no taller than five feet eight inches, and that he weighed well in excess of three hundred pounds.

Kelly smiled and sipped his wine, remembering the solemn vow he had made to himself more than twenty years earlier.

After he had lost everything.

CHAPTER 4

The Innocent

T h e girls had loved the Twinkies.

Betty and Veronica, LaVerne and Shirley and all the others. Every last one of them.

They were good girls.

Johnny had made them good.

He sat on the floor surrounded by them and licked the sweet white filling of the last Twinkie from his fingers. Betty and Veronica had giggled shyly when he had offered it to them to share, insisting that he take it instead. The others had joined in then, reminding him how hard he worked to take care of them all, saving his money to buy them special treats.

That's the kind of girls they were.

All of them, that is, except Diana. He looked up from the battered brown sofa where he had been comfortably thumbing through a mail-order lingerie catalog by the light of the Coleman lantern—his head on Shirley's shoulder, his feet propped on Lois's lap—and saw her staring at him from the damp corner; the corner where he put them when they were being naughty. Deep shadows fell across the sunken sockets of her eyes and he knew she was trying to frighten him again.

He hoped she wouldn't start talking to him. It scared him when she talked. None of the other girls ever talked without his permission, and when they did it was only to say nice things. Things that came to him in his head. Things he wanted them to say.

Only Diana said the other things to him: the bad things about how terrible he was and how it was wrong of him to keep bringing more and more girls here, girls he should have left alone. When she spoke, he could hear her with his ears.

That was what frightened him.

He thought about getting up and going to her before she started talking, maybe taking away the pretty red nightgown he had ordered especially for her so she wouldn't be so sad and angry about the things he'd had to do to her on that long-ago Christmas Eve, things he'd only done to make her good and make the bad thing stop happening.

He had tried to explain to her that night—stammering and stuttering as he held her down on the floor of the pickup—wanting her to understand about the bad thing and his mother and the golden star. But she wouldn't listen; had screamed and kicked at him instead, trying to get the door open. Calling over and over for the boy she had been with to come and save her.

He'd finally had to hurt her to make her be quiet—he didn't want to hurt her. Never wanted to hurt any of his girls. Sometimes, though, they made him do it.

It wasn't his fault.

Johnny turned his eyes back to his catalog, pointing out a lacy garter belt to Shirley. He saw the light gleaming dully in her eyes and folded the page over. Pretty soon it would be her birthday. He knew that because he'd looked it up in the records room at the Bremerton city hall soon after he'd brought her home a few months earlier. He winked at her, teasing, and her soft tinkling giggle sounded inside his head. Maybe he'd buy it for her if she was extra specially good.

He noticed the dab of white filling on her chin and reached up to wipe it off, picking up his can of orange soda and pouring a little bit into her mouth. It dribbled out the corner and he shook his head. Shirley was so clumsy. All the girls were. He couldn't imagine what they would do without him.

Diana was still staring at him from the dark corner and he thought briefly about what he would do if she started talking again. He would have to punish her, maybe even put her in the cold room. He didn't want to have to do that. It was dark and lonely in the cold room and the girls he put there hardly ever came out again.

Diana gazed silently at him, but she did not say anything.

Johnny was glad.

She had been with him the longest and in many ways he was prouder of her than all the others.

CHAPTER 5

Rules of Engagement

KELLY had quickly come to realize that his Vietnam experience had been entirely uncommon in that he had never come any closer to any of the men—or women—he had killed than did the navy pilots who indiscriminately strafed and bombed "suspected" Viet Cong positions before returning to clean sheets and videotaped movies aboard the giant aircraft carriers that continuously prowled the South China Sea.

Compared to the flyboys, he had been as innocent in his slaughter as a newborn baby. For the powerful telescopic sights mounted on his match-quality sniper's rifle had always defined in minute detail his target's distinctive black Viet Cong uniforms, their Chinese-manufactured AK47s, and the portable Russian rockets they carried over their shoulders.

Very early in his tour, during which he was left almost entirely to his own devices, he had devised the simple set of criteria by which he determined who would live and who would die. Only those Vietnamese wearing black pajamas *and* carrying weapons were designated as targets, and then *only* if they were observed moving surreptitiously through the rice paddies or fields—instead of on the roads—very early in the morning or around dusk. Those were typical patterns practiced only by the enemy and individuals not meeting all three tests lived.

The rest he considered evil by definition and thus in need of killing.

The young sniper's standards occasionally clashed with official demands for increased body counts, but the way Chris had it figured, the major back in his air-conditioned hooch in Da Nang didn't have to watch the heads of the Cong he executed exploding like overripe watermelons in his scope. Chris Kelly did, and he would be damned if he was going to lie awake nights wondering if he'd mistakenly wasted some poor mama-san carrying a bundle of sticks to her rice paddy. And if the major didn't like it he could damn well court-martial him, or send him home.

Fat fucking chance.

After having witnessed numerous examples of the enemy's brutality to the hapless civilian population, it had occurred to Kelly that he had been sent to Vietnam for only one reason: to kill bad guys. To wipe evil from the face of the earth.

On the increasingly rare occasions when he allowed himself to ponder the riddle of Diana's disappearance—as opposed to his sweet memories of their innocent love—her shadowy abductor wore black pajamas and enforced his will with an AK47.

It made the killing that much easier.

Although Kelly, unlike the navy flyboys, had no secure floating refuge to call home during the two years and six days of his tenure in the Vietnamese highlands—despite the one-year rotation rule, at the end of his normal tour the major had declared him "an essential technical specialist" and kept him working until the last days of his enlistment. He had developed and employed a dozen skills related to survival and evasion, the practice of which soon became as natural and effortless to him as had his boyhood ability to blend into each of the two dozen different schools he had attended on far-flung military bases around the world.

Except for the killing, which he forbade himself to think about very much, Chris Kelly could have actually enjoyed his time in Vietnam.

Returning to the Warmbad guesthouse after an excellent dinner of lamb done up in tender grape leaves, he showered, dressed, and stretched out on the bed for a few hours of rest. Although the thirty-hour trip from New York had given him ample time to nap, the airplane seat hadn't been built that could replace the luxury of a soft bed.

He lay awake until nearly midnight, going over the details of the drive he would soon be making to a deserted village called Mabula. His plan called for him to stash the BMW in an abandoned machinery shed near the village, check his equipment, then proceed on foot to a kopje, or hilltop, overlooking the compound where Saleem's meeting was to take place.

If the assassination—a single explosive round to the head from a silenced small-bore match rifle—went off flawlessly, and they almost always did, he would simply walk back to the BMW, return to the motorway, and drive north to Swaziland, where he planned to wrap up the weekend in the casinos before returning to Jo'burg for a Monday morning meeting with the manager of a well-known black recording artist.

Saleem's death, if it was reported at all, would inspire little more than relief among South African authorities, who, for all their former repression of the black majority, had always been fanatical about maintaining their image as the guardians of African wildlife.

Whatever personal danger Kelly faced would come from Saleem's bodyguards, and, perhaps, those of the arms dealer. There were several alternate plans in the event of trouble, including the unlikely prospect of an overland crossing to Zimbabwe. But beyond having specified that his equipment include a small pack filled with basic camping supplies, and having brought along the lightweight hiking boots that he intended to wear on the mission, he felt fairly certain he would be breakfasting back in Warmbad before Saleem's guards discovered where the silenced shot had come from. It was more likely they would all cut and run at the first sign of trouble. The penalties for both poaching and illegal arms dealing in South Africa could be charitably described as draconian at best.

Having gone over the physical details of his plan as best he could, he glanced at the Rolex. The luminous dial showed that it was nearly midnight. There were three hours remaining before he left the guesthouse.

He plumped the large pillows up against the headboard, folded his hands behind his head, and wondered briefly which of the several governments anxious to be rid of Muktar Saleem had actually contracted with Harvest Media for his death. It would have had to be one friendly to the United States, as all Harvest contracts had to be investigated and approved by the tribunal, a revolving panel that was largely funded by the United States and made up of current and retired jurists from six nations.

Kelly shrugged and went to sleep. It wasn't any of his business, he supposed.

Returning briefly to Bremerton at the venerable age of twenty-two, Chris Kelly had quickly learned the hard way that the very fact of his military service, much less the details of his particular Vietnam experience, was a shameful thing. Some would even have labeled what he had done as an atrocity.

His mother had passed away while he was in the service and his father, who had taken to drinking heavily, had retired from the army with vague grandiose plans to use his pension to purchase and restore a rambling clapboard hotel at a nearby mountain lake to the grandeur it had enjoyed in the twenties and thirties.

The project had failed before the doors ever opened, driving his father to the brink of bankruptcy and reducing his inheritance when the old man died of drink a few years later to sixty acres of heavily forested ground surrounding the boarded-up hotel.

With no reason to stay, and feeling cheated and betrayed by the country whose flag he had been raised to honor above all things, Kelly had left the property, which he had never actually set foot on, to be looked after by his married cousin, Shelly, and her husband, and traveled west to enroll in the premed program at Stanford University in California. There he had set valiantly to work, determined to erase the stain of all the little faceless Vietnamese men and women he had so trustingly wasted in the name of democracy and freedom.

His last act before leaving Bremerton had been a visit to the shady hillside cemetery where he had solemnly vowed on the graves of his parents and the memory of his beloved Diana never to kill anyone again, even at the expense of his own life.

Diana.

He felt cheated that there was nothing left of her to remember; not even a stone above a grave.

Nothing but the dull ache in his heart.

He had stayed at Stanford for two years, struggling all the while against the unfamiliar demands of a grueling academic schedule for which his Marine Corps experience had scarcely prepared him. His grades began to fall early in his sophomore year and, doubting more profoundly with each passing day that his dreams of expiating his profound guilt through the expedient of becoming a healer of broken bodies would ever be realized, he began to consider what else he might do with his life.

That was when Mr. Black had looked him up.

Isaac Blackstone—Mr. Black to the employees of Harvest Media Productions—was a gentle, scholarly man in his late forties who had simply appeared at the door of his tiny off-campus apartment one evening, claiming to be a recruiter of "exceptional young talent."

Something in the soft tone of Blackstone's voice and the way he wore the baggy tweed suit, the pants legs of which dropped over the tops of his scuffed brown oxfords, suggested he might have something interesting to say and the bleary-eyed student had let him in, despite the fact that he was sweating a crucial chemistry exam early the next morning. Blackstone's pitch, however, was disappointing. Kelly had listened for fifteen minutes as the older man vaguely described Harvest's excellent employee benefits program with growing certitude that it was he who was being evaluated, and not Harvest Media, whatever in the hell that was.

About the company's actual purpose and activities, Blackstone would say little more than that Harvest was dedicated to making the world a better place through the production of cultural programs, the proceeds of which were directed to various charitable purposes. Although he hinted that making the world a better place occasionally involved certain other "opportunistic activities," he was very nonspecific about what those activities might be and Kelly had politely but firmly ushered him to the door, adding that he might well be interested in employment, but that for the moment his chemistry exam was king of the hill. Blackstone had smiled at that, and left after shaking Kelly's hand, thanking him for his time and promising to contact him again in the near future.

The following afternoon, Kelly had been sitting in the student union silently bemoaning the fact that he had miserably busted the chemistry exam, and wishing he had thought to ask Blackstone for his card, when the old gentleman had magically reappeared at his side.

He took the glum student to lunch at an expensive restaurant and had sat watching over the tops of his smudged horn-rimmed glasses as Kelly consumed martini after martini, the liquor eventually loosening his tongue to the extent that he ended up venting all his frustrations at his seemingly foiled attempt to atone for the dozens of unknown men and women he had killed.

When he had finally stopped talking, Blackstone looked at him, his pale gray eyes burning with a hidden passion the younger man could not begin to fathom.

"Yet some men truly do deserve to die," he had said in his quiet, slightly accented voice. "Consider how usefully your exceptional talents might have been employed by a caring, just government working not for political or commercial ends, but in the honest concern of eradicating truly evil men from the earth, and of those only the ones who wreak the greatest misery upon humankind."

"No, goddammit!" Kelly had slurred the response to the theoretical question, casting his eyes down to the food that still lay untouched on his plate. "Nothing can justify that kind of killing."

"Yes," the older man had insisted, pulling back the sleeve of his worn tweed jacket to expose a pale, veined forearm. "Consider the men who did this to me, for instance. I was just a schoolboy. I watched helplessly as those men brutally murdered thousands of innocents; Jews, priests, the mentally ill. . . . Wouldn't you agree that the deaths of such men as those are justified?"

Kelly had stared at the series of crude blue

numbers etched into Blackstone's pale skin for a long time. "What if some of the men who tattooed you were like me," he finally stammered, "following orders in the mistaken belief that what they were doing was right at the time, no matter how wrong it may have proven to be in retrospect?"

"Then it would be incumbent upon such men to honorably acquit themselves by dedicating themselves to fighting evil to the absolute best of their abilities, once they had discovered the error of their ways, wouldn't it?" Blackstone had replied with irrefutable logic.

"You mean killing people, don't you?"

Blackstone had nodded slowly, stroking his short, gray mustache with fingers that Kelly had suddenly noticed with horror were devoid of nails. "*Executing* them, yes," he had replied, seeming not to notice that the younger man was staring at his hands. "But cleanly and humanely and, even then, only those who are indisputably deserving of it."

"Ah, and who decides that?" Kelly had smiled at him then for the first time, smug in the sophomoric assurance that he had finally trapped Blackstone in the web of his own flawed rhetoric.

"Why, you do," he had replied.

"Me?"

"Yes." He had smiled triumphantly, revealing a set of poorly fitted dentures.

"You, the executioner."

CHAPTER 6

Bedtime

I T was getting late.

The protests of the girls jangled inside his head as he stood and made the announcement.

Laughing and waggling his finger at them, Johnny began rearranging them according to size and weight, lifting Shirley and Lois and carrying them gently in to their beds, brotherly kisses planted on each pretty nose.

Returning to the living room, he repeated the procedure, tucking warm blankets around Betty and Veronica's pretty legs, bestowing more kisses. Finally, he carried Diana unprotesting into the sleeping room and placed her on a small cot in the corner. He bent over and whispered into her ear, telling her that he was happy she had finally decided to be good again.

She said nothing.

Satisfied that all was well, he sniffed the air

suspiciously. The hours he had spent scrubbing the sleeping room with disinfectant had been worth the effort. Things were always in such an awful mess when he had returned after so many days away from the girls.

Many more hours had been spent tending to each of them individually. He hoped he would never have to stay away from them so long again.

Smiling to himself, he pulled the long string running from the naked bulb on the ceiling—the refuge's only electrical outlet—and the room was plunged into darkness.

He turned and tiptoed out, closing the door softly behind him. Laverne was alone in the living room, the sequins on her pretty prom dress sparkling like magic in the soft light of the lantern.

Johnny sat down beside her and shyly placed a pudgy hand on her knee. "H-hi," he said. "Y-ya want an orange soda?" He felt the bad thing pressing against the coarse material of his overalls, but it no longer bothered him as it once had.

Being with one of his pretty, pretty girls always made the bad thing go away.

He leaned over to plant a clumsy kiss on her cheek and sniffed the faint unpleasant odor beneath her heavy, flower-scented perfume.

Very soon he would need to find a new girl.

C H A P T E R   7

Wakeup

T H E guest house was, as Kelly had anticipated, silent at three A.M. Leaving a note at the
small desk explaining that he was anxious to get
on to his next destination in advance of the
weekend traffic, he walked out into the chill
night air and wiped a thin layer of mist from the
BMW's windshield.

Going around to the trunk, he opened it and
tossed his small overnight case inside. A large
Louis Vuitton suitcase that had not been there
when he had arrived in Warmbad filled the compact space. Working in the illumination of the
trunk light, he quickly zipped open the case and
examined the contents of the dark blue nylon
backpack inside: envelopes of freeze-dried food,
two liters of water in plastic bottles, a knife, a
small first-aid kit, a ground cloth and a nine-
millimeter Beretta automatic pistol with two

spare clips of ammunition completed his emergency supplies.

He gave the Beretta a quick but thorough
examination, slipped it and the spare clips into
his jacket pockets, and set the backpack aside.
Beneath it, a molded plastic case of matte black
plastic filled the bottom of the suitcase. Flipping
the catches on the lid, he opened it to reveal the
components of a disassembled .225-caliber rifle
of Belgian manufacture nestled in deep bur-
gundy velvet. The rifle's machined sound sup-
pressor and preshimmed fifty-power scope with
snap-on mount gleamed dully in separate com-
partments, as did the half dozen rounds of
explosive-tipped ammunition. Satisfied that
everything was precisely as specified on the
detailed requisition he had filled out in
Arlington six days earlier, he snapped the gun
case shut, replaced the backpack, and zipped
up the suitcase.

Kelly had no earthly idea how the suitcase
had gotten into the locked trunk of the car, nor
did he need or want to know. It was a hard and
fast rule at Harvest that such things were
"arranged" as required. An unknown logistics
operative would collect the equipment when he
was through with it. That, too, was none of his
affair.

The BMW's engine purred instantly to life at
the turn of the key and he pulled out of the
gravel car park, pointing the automobile toward
the dry, rolling hills to the west. As promised by
the tourist map, the pavement abruptly ended

at the town limits, replaced by a smoothly graded dirt road that swept past scattered farmhouses and isolated stands of scrub and lion grass. His route would take him into the foothills of a forbidding range of dry mountains where he would turn off onto a narrow track for the last leg of his drive.

He fiddled with the radio as he drove, finally picking up a weak signal from the government-run SABC station in Praetoria. The speedometer needle hovered around the hundred-and-twenty-kilometer mark as he drummed his fingers to the latest Michael Jackson tune and wondered if he would really be able to shoot Saleem from the security of heavy cover at five hundred meters as the terrain mockups and reconnaissance photos he had reviewed after personally approving the target suggested he might.

CHAPTER 8

The Killing

MUKTAR Saleem was, as advertised, fat and oily. A mountain of flesh draped in a tentlike robe of some fine gray cloth, the flesh-peddler-turned-drug-lord glided down the folding stairway of the black Aerospatiale helicopter and stood looking disdainfully about the dirt clearing as a squad of swarthy men in well-cut business suits fanned out about the ramshackle boma.

The helicopter was a variation of the familiar French military model, although Kelly had never seen one configured quite like it before. It had swung in low from the north a few moments earlier, flying below treetop level without lights. The whisper of its rotors indicated that the machine was a specially modified stealth model and its high-speed, low-level approach in the predawn darkness suggested that the pilot was equipped with night-vision goggles. It was a lot of high-tech gadgetry for a private aircraft.

Figure fifteen or twenty million U.S. dollars' worth, he thought.

The sun was just peeking over the range of low, arid mountains to the east, backlighting his target perfectly in the modified sniperscope.

Kelly scrunched down in his hiding place atop the steep southern face of the kopje, waiting to see if his contact would come out to meet Saleem, having been promised a bonus if he could, so to speak, kill two birds with one stone. He clicked the scope optics down to eight power, affording himself a broader view of the clearing and doubting that he would be able to identify the second target before the fat man started moving, although he mentally complimented the unknown planner who had chosen this shooting perch for him. Three hundred meters distant from and twenty meters above the killing field, his sheltered nest atop the kopje presented a sheer rock face to any would-be pursuers while allowing him an easy retreat down the same trail he had followed up the hill's gently sloping backside.

All he had to do now was pop the target with a single silent shot and walk away.

No one had yet appeared from within the poorly maintained wattles of the boma compound and the bodyguards, having poked the muzzles of their Uzis into the various nooks and crannies surrounding the clearing, were moving back in on Saleem. Kelly clicked the scope onto a higher power, gaining an extreme close-up of the fat man's face. Individual drops of sweat popped into sharp focus on his forehead as his piggish eyes darted suspiciously here and there.

Time to shoot.

He had aligned the crosshairs perfectly on the thick bridge of Saleem's nose and was squeezing down ever so gently on the trigger . . . when the fat man suddenly moved, swinging his head around to look back at the helicopter, and presenting the sniper a blurred ripple of patterned cloth as the traditional Arab headpiece he was wearing swirled across his field of vision.

Cursing softly, Kelly clicked back to eight power and saw that some activity had broken out beside the helicopter. As he watched, a young Caucasian girl of perhaps twelve or thirteen jumped from the open door and ran toward the surrounding bush, her naked legs flashing ghostly white in the growing light.

Someone yelled, the sound drifting faintly up to where Kelly lay hidden, and the nearest bodyguard raised his Uzi. A bright rosette of light twinkled from the stubby black barrel of the machine gun and the girl fell in a dusty cloud at the very edge of the clearing, her blond hair tangled in the branches of a thorn bush. Kelly clicked his scope back onto a close-up of Saleem in time to see the evil smile creasing the obscene folds of fat in which his face was encased, and lined up the shot a second time.

If he had previously entertained any doubts about this job—which required him to kill a man whose photo he had never even seen, something he normally refused to do—they had vanished in the instant the girl fell.

The thought flashed through his mind that dying was far too good for this bastard.

A bodyguard stepped into his line of fire and Kelly waited for him to move, using the opportunity to flex the tense muscles of his trigger hand and taking several deep breaths in order to slow his racing pulse. He had long ago learned never to allow himself to become impatient about these things.

He was fully committed to killing Muktar Saleem.

"*I'm* to decide who dies?"

Kelly had stared openmouthed at Blackstone the night the Holocaust survivor had explained that Kelly, the executioner, would decide which of his targets was to die, unable to envision himself pursuing a career that once again required him to make such choices as a matter of routine. In practice, however, it turned out that Harvest's system of running its assassinations program was brilliantly simple, and as nearly foolproof as any such enterprise could be.

Harvest Media, an organization truly dedicated to ridding the world of evil, allowed its assassins—informally referred to as reapers—full and final participation in all targeting decisions. The logic behind this unique practice was, according to Blackstone, that the physical danger of the assassination would be borne by the reaper alone and the blood of targeted individuals on their hands. Therefore, the reapers—all of whom had been selected for their honest dedication to improving the human condition, as well as for proven skills in the killing arts—should be accorded the final option of whether or not to carry out a given assignment.

Targets were selected based upon data independently compiled by the organization's own investigative branch following formal requests from one of several authorized governmental organizations, and approved by an international panel of retired jurists.

Once a target had been approved by the panel, his or her entire file (Harvest were equal-opportunity killers) along with any additional data that might be requested by the reaper, was presented to the assassin for final review. Throughout the process, a highly skilled pleader, Harvest's version of a defense attorney, was on hand to argue and defend even the smallest points in favor of the proposed target being allowed to continue living.

It had sounded at first like a system that might leave a man with a lot of sleepless nights. In practice, however, Kelly had found that the small number of cases that actually reached the stage of being assigned to individual reapers seldom left even an iota of doubt as to the target's qualifications for termination. In his time, he had reviewed the cases of drug kingpins, psychopathic dictators, and rabid terrorists, and only once had he turned down a target—an ailing Mafia lieutenant who, he had inadvertently discovered while preparing to kill the man, was already dying of cancer.

The final decision to kill was always left in the hands of the reaper, who was free to reject the target for any reason whatsoever, at any time up to the moment of actual termination.

Reapers' decisions were final, and once a target had been rejected, he or she was dropped from consideration for assassination for a minimum of three years.

The bodyguard moved away and Saleem began waddling toward the boma, where a shadowy figure stood in the doorway awaiting him. Kelly lined the fat man up in his sights once more.

A small breeze suddenly arose, sweeping across the clearing in a series of tiny whirlwinds. Saleem's headdress flapped about his face, spoiling Kelly's aim a second time and he cursed under his breath, wanting the head shot but unable to guarantee it. The Arab was no more than twenty paces from the safety of the boma now. Another ten seconds and he would be home free. Unless he wanted to risk lying up in the rocks for however long Saleem's meeting with the arms dealer would take—which would mean shooting in full daylight with all the attendant dangers—Kelly had to take him now.

With a shot to the heart.

Anyone who has killed more than a few men,

or animals for that matter, knows that the head shot is always preferable to any other. In this instance, with the heavy explosive bullet in his chamber, a hit anywhere on the skull virtually guaranteed Kelly a clean kill. Body shots, on the other hand, were notoriously unreliable. The shot might hit something vital and it might not. The difficulty of assuring a kill with a shot to the body was greatly compounded on a man as massive as Saleem. Also, there was always the chance that the target could be wearing body armor beneath his clothing.

Ten paces separated Saleem from the safety of the boma. It had to be now or not at all.

This man had to die.

Kelly clicked his optics back to a lower power, dropped the sights to the middle of Saleem's massive chest, and squeezed.

The noise-suppressed rifle popped with the intensity of a heavy book being dropped onto a desktop from a height of six or eight inches, a small sound that was lost among the chirping of the birds about the kopje.

In the clearing below, a bright red hole blossomed in the center of Muktar Saleem's chest. Kelly allowed himself a grim smile—Saleem had not been wearing body armor after all—and waited for him to drop. His mind was already turning to the details of his escape: a brisk walk down to the stand of acacia trees below the kopje, where he would drop the disassembled rifle into a predug hole and kick dirt and leaves over it before stepping directly into the dry streambed that led back to the shed housing the BMW.

Two or three seconds passed and he was still staring through the sights. Saleem stood in the clearing before the boma, looking down intently at his bloody chest. But he remained standing.

Clicking his scope onto its highest power, Chris Kelly gazed into Saleem's open wound. Shards of fractured cartilage gleamed yellow in the morning light around the perimeter of the glistening, fist-sized hole in his chest. Streams of blood gushed down the front of the gray robe, obscenely plastering the thin material to the fat man's protruding belly. As he watched, a pudgy hand bedecked with sparkling rings touched the raw meat at the edge of the hole. A thick finger probed at the jagged wound.

Kelly should have been halfway down the backside of the kopje by that time, but he could not will himself to move.

Something was horribly, unaccountably wrong. Something that his brain could not rightly absorb.

Hands trembling with the effort, he raised the telescopic sight to Saleem's face. The swarthy features were contorted, whether in agony or in anger Kelly could not tell, and he was still gazing down at himself.

Saleem suddenly raised his head and looked straight up into the lens of the telescopic sight, his black, beady eyes glittering with hatred in the morning light, and although he could not possibly have seen the assassin, sequestered as he was among the rocks and shadows of the kopje, Kelly felt those eyes boring into his very soul.

The moment ended as Saleem dropped abruptly out of sight, and Kelly took his eye from the lens to look down into the clearing. The fat man was being carried into the helicopter by two men in suits. The brisk crackle of automatic gunfire rattled across the veld as the three remaining bodyguards began indiscriminately spraying the flimsy walls of the boma with their weapons.

Kelly got to his feet and ran then, unable to comprehend what had just occurred.

There was no way Muktar Saleem could have survived the killing shot he had just placed in the center of his chest.

It was not humanly possible.

The muffled, whacking sound of the Aerospatiale's main rotors echoed off the rocks behind him as he dived into the acacia thicket at the foot of the kopje and hastily broke down the rifle. Dumping the pieces into the shallow hole he had dug earlier for the purpose, he kicked a few inches of dry earth over them and dragged a splintered branch across the excavation.

It wasn't much but it would have to do.

The sound of the helicopter grew louder and he peered out from the trees in time to see it clear the rim of the kopje and bear away to the north, clawing for altitude.

Good.

At least he didn't have to concern himself

about a pursuit from the air, a pursuit against which he would be practically defenseless. Saleem's bodyguards must have decided that their first priority was to get their boss clear of the area in case there were more shooters around.

A wise choice.

He heard shouts far off to his left, and the sound of an engine starting. He wasn't anxious to discover whether this signaled the beginning of a ground search for him or the arms dealer's decision to evacuate the bullet-riddled boma. Taking a deep breath and patting his hand against the hard, comforting outline of the pistol in his pocket, he peered out of the thicket, scanning the terrain around the kopje for signs of danger.

Nothing.

He quickly ducked back into the protective shadows of the acacias and, following a narrow game track that required him to duck beneath low-hanging branches, made his way to the opposite edge of the small stand of trees. He paused again to check the dry creek that ambled past the thicket's western border. Seeing nothing, he stepped onto the sandy creek bottom and moved away at a brisk walk.

As he walked, Kelly tried not to think about the grisly hole in Saleem's chest, concentrating his attention instead on scanning the way ahead for signs of an impending ambush.

The way was clear.

He knew in his heart that there had to be

some rational explanation for those few seconds in which Saleem had refused to fall.

He just couldn't think of one.

"When you have ruled out the impossible, whatever remains, however improbable, must be the truth."

Blackstone was very fond of Sherlock Holmes, liberally peppering his lectures with quotes from the fictional sleuth in what Kelly had at first supposed was an attempt to keep his subjects from nodding off. The quotes were, he had later discovered, a carefully designed part of Blackstone's rigid program for making his young protégés think about things, everyday things that ordinary people with ordinary jobs were allowed to take for granted.

Rule One: Reapers never take anything for granted.

The automatic was in his hand as he stepped cautiously out of the creek bed.

He carefully circled the abandoned shed, keeping well to the cover of the surrounding bush.

The shed appeared exactly as he had left it.

Breaking cover at a crouch, he slipped into the tumbledown building through a low side door and stood in the darkness listening to the pounding of his own heart. The BMW's silver paint gleamed in the stray shafts of sunlight that poured in through the cracks in the weathered siding. The car appeared undisturbed. Kelly relaxed slightly and cautiously stepped toward the right-side driver's door.

"It's perfectly all right," said a deep voice from the shadows beyond the car. "They've all gone."

Dropping instinctively to the ground, Kelly rolled under a wooden bench laden with rusted buckets, simultaneously chambering a round into the pistol.

"That's really not necessary," said the voice. There was movement near the right front fender and a tall black man stepped into the dim light, hands raised above his head.

"Who are you?" Kelly croaked.

"Your logistics officer," he said, stepping closer and smiling to reveal a line of perfectly white teeth set in a remarkably handsome face of classic Zulu proportions. "It was I who placed the rifle in the boot of your car last night, and I who shall retrieve it from the spot where you have buried it."

"Don't come any closer," Kelly warned.

He had never before met a logistics officer. Not even in training. It was an ironclad rule among reapers that you never met anyone you could get into trouble, and vice versa. The stuff you needed was just where it was supposed to be when you needed it. Somebody took care of it afterward, as required. That was all you were supposed to know. Having somebody show up in the middle of an assignment claiming to be his logistics officer was frightening.

"What do you want?" Kelly demanded. He could see now that the black man was dressed in ragged khakis and a Grateful Dead T-shirt. Somehow he had always assumed that logistics officers were Ivy League types drawn from the ranks of junior embassy staff.

This guy did not fit the profile.

"I know it's a major breach of protocol," the man said, "but I've been lying up in the bush waiting to retrieve your weapon. I heard a great deal of shooting and saw the helicopter leave. . . ."

He hesitated, tilting his head in the general direction of the killing ground. "I thought perhaps you might tell me what happened before I go stumbling in there to retrieve your weapon."

"I'll tell you what happened," Kelly replied, getting to his feet while still keeping the gun trained on the stranger. "The target—"

"Saleem," the man interrupted, "Muktar Saleem."

"The target," Kelly repeated through clenched teeth, "has been terminated."

He waved the pistol at the black man again, indicating that he wanted him to move away from the car. The man held his ground. "Then you hit him?" he said.

"I don't fucking miss targets," Kelly spat, kicking open the shed door at the rear of the car and moving to the driver's door. "It just took a second for him to fall."

The black man backed away as he yanked open the car door and slid behind the wheel. "I'm very sorry. I tried to tell them," he said, sticking his head in through the passenger side window.

Kelly stared at him. "You tried to tell them what?"

"About Saleem. That they could not kill him like this, with rifles. Of course they laughed at me."

The pistol suddenly began to tremble uncontrollably in Kelly's hand. "I hit him clean," he said, and heard his voice crack. "Center shot."

"It wasn't your fault," the man said. He placed his hand on top of the pistol barrel and gently pushed it down onto the seat. "You couldn't have known."

"But I hit him, center shot," Kelly insisted.

"Of course you did." He nodded sympathetically. "But that would have made no difference. You see, Muktar Saleem cannot be killed. He is protected by a powerful spell."

Kelly suppressed a hysterical giggle. "A spell?"

The man's handsome head bobbed up and down and his eyes seemed to widen in the faint light of the BMW's dashboard. "It is well known to everyone in this district. I tried to warn them not to send you. . . ."

Reality suddenly snapped the assassin's brain back into its proper place. "Okay, pal," he said, reaching down to crank the BMW's ignition key, "you tried to warn them. I gotta go now. You take care."

The powerful engine roared to life and he moved the gearshift into reverse.

"But you don't understand," the man pleaded. His head and shoulders were still protruding into the car through the open window. "You are in great danger now."

Kelly revved the engine and eased out the clutch, causing the car to lurch backward a few inches.

"You're the one who's in great danger, pal, 'cause in exactly three seconds I'm gonna back out of here, with or without your head stuck in my window."

The other man jerked his head out of the car as Kelly hit the throttle. The car screeched out of the shed in reverse. He slammed on the brakes, wrenched the wheel around toward the dirt track he'd arrived on, and shoved the shift lever into first gear.

"They will place a curse on you," screamed the black man into the dust thrown up by the spinning tires. "Great misfortune will surely fall upon you now."

"Fuck you and the horse you rode in on," Kelly yelled as the powerful car rocketed away into the orange ball of the rising African sun. "Shock," he mumbled to himself, the shock of the bullet's impact had left the target standing for a moment. That was all.

CHAPTER 9

Window Shopping

JOHNNY loved malls.

Their bright, open spaces and strolling crowds provided almost limitless opportunities to watch girls, who flocked by the hundreds to the theaters and shops and restaurants, parading past him in an endlessly enticing array of shapely limbs and bottoms.

He had discovered that if he carried a shopping bag and maintained the slightly weary look of the bored husbands waiting for their wives to finish their endless rounds of shopping in the mall, he could sit unmolested for hours at a time at one of the many tables near the fast-food places, eating and smoking and sipping orange sodas while he graded and evaluated the quality and skin tone of the girls presented for his inspection.

Skin tone, he had come to realize after several

horribly botched attempts—failures that he had regrettably been forced to consign to the cold room after a few weeks or days—was absolutely critical to keeping his girls sweet and pretty. While he very much preferred girls with fair, thin skin and light hair, they were always the hardest to get right, bruising and discoloring at the slightest mistake. That was one reason he was still so proud of Diana. She had been his first, and although her hair and skin were exceedingly fine, she had turned out perfectly.

The mall he had chosen today, Penn Center, was one of the newest in the two-hundred-mile radius of Johnny's primary shopping grounds. Since its grand opening less than a year earlier, the gleaming complex had become one of his favorites—both Shirley and Lois had come from Penn Center.

Located off a busy interstate highway just north of Philadelphia, and less than eighty miles from home, the gigantic shopping complex featured a multilevel underground parking structure whose myriad entrances and exits were ideal for Johnny's purposes.

A pair of giggling teenagers passed by within a few feet of the table he was occupying and he carefully scrutinized them from behind the long bill of the local lumber company baseball cap he wore pulled low over his eyes. He liked the baseball cap, which disguised his features while making him look like just another working stiff from one of the numerous industrial complexes in the surrounding area.

The cap was much better than the sunglasses he'd once tried. Sunglasses, he'd quickly learned, made people suspicious of you, especially when you wore them indoors. People were always suspicious if they couldn't see your eyes.

His eyes followed the girls to a bank of escalators leading down to the parking structure. The taller of the two, a pretty brunette with full red lips and a waist-length ponytail, was very nice, but he did not pick up his shopping bag to follow her.

Johnny only followed girls who departed the main floor of the mall by themselves, trailing them from a discreet distance to see which level of the parking structure they would enter. If he was very lucky, they would proceed to the same one he'd parked the truck on. He preferred the middle levels, which he had found tended to be darker and noisier than the top ones. The very bottom levels—which made the girls nervous and were thus patrolled more heavily by mall security guards and provided fewer exits—he avoided altogether.

If the girl he had chosen went on to another level, he might follow just to see what kind of car she was driving. Girls driving low-slung sports cars, he had discovered, often hiked up their skirts once they were behind the wheel, affording him tantalizing glimpses of their thighs as they drove past. But, other than looking, he left them alone.

The success of his shopping almost always depended on the girl entering the same level where he had strategically parked the truck, allowing him to hurry past and dangle the irresistible lure that almost always drew her over to him for a closer look. Very occasionally, he would reverse the process, waiting in the truck until a suitable girl drove into the garage, then maneuvering into a parking space near her vehicle to await her return. This was harder, and posed the added risk of drawing the attention of his enemies, the mall security guards, who were constantly buzzing up and down the ramps in their funny little electric carts.

Catching girls the way Johnny did was a very slow and time-consuming process. There might be other people in the garage, or the girl might hurry to her car, oblivious to his lure. None of this bothered him in the slightest degree. For, just like the forest creatures whose cunning survival skills he so admired and mimicked, he was possessed of infinite patience.

CHAPTER 10

The Long Way Home

THE return trip to the States was uneventful.

Unnerved by the sudden appearance of the black man claiming to be his logistics officer, Kelly scrapped the planned side trip to Swaziland and drove north into Zimbabwe. Flashing a fresh passport at the bored customs officials at the border and pausing long enough to lunch at Victoria Falls, he pressed on to Harare where he caught another Swissair flight bound for Zurich via Nairobi.

He hung around the Zurich airport for a couple of hours, taking advantage of the layover to shower and shave in one of the weird ultraviolet sanitary booths the Swiss provide for weary travelers, dug out a third passport and finally boarded a Pan Am flight to Kennedy that was filled with American tourists dressed in lederhosen and hats sprouting funny little brushes.

Exhausted and shaken by his experience, he nodded off once on the flight, the muffled roar of the 747's engines blending into the sound of the big waterfall up the mountain at his grandfather's favorite fishing hole. In his dream, he and the old man, whom he had always called Pop, were fishing below the falls, shouting at each other to be heard over the roar and laughing at some joke they shared. Suddenly, Pop lifted his rod and pointed and Kelly turned his head to see a dark form taking shape behind the gleaming curtain of the waterfall. He stared transfixed as the waters parted and the image of Muktar Saleem materialized into his dream. The fat man looked down sadly at his ravaged chest, then raised his eyes and spread his bloody hands wide. "Why have you done this to me?" he keened in a high-pitched voice. "I have done nothing to you, ever."

"Go away," screamed Kelly. "You're dead."

The apparition vanished and Kelly turned to see Pop shaking his head in amusement, the fishing lures stuck into the band of his old floppy hat sparkling in the sunlight. "There's dead and then there's *dead,*" chuckled the old man, pointing his rod again. "Not all of 'em stay that way."

Kelly stared at the old man in puzzlement, then followed his gaze back to the waterfall. Dozens of dark figures were massing behind the shimmering curtain. A hand appeared through the water, the arm above clad in a black pajama sleeve. . . .

He came instantly awake, flailing out with his arms and upsetting a drink into the lap of the hopelessly drab little schoolteacher in the next seat. He remembered that he had been rude to her when they had first boarded the plane in Zurich, having rebuffed her bright attempt at conversation by burying his head in a pillow and staring out the window. Now, by way of atonement he bought her a fresh drink and listened to her breathless account of the alpine walking tour she had just completed. He listened until the plane mercifully landed in New York at two in the afternoon.

He grabbed a shuttle to Washington National and stared out the dirty window for the duration of the brief flight.

Saleem was still nagging at him.

He should have died instantly.

No one was waiting for him in Washington. But then, no one ever was. The old Ford Escort he retained exclusively for trips to the airport was sitting right where he had left it, its windows streaked with several days' accumulation of dirt and the left front tire looking a little flatter than he remembered. He got in, coaxed the balky engine to life, and briefly considered fighting the flow of Friday afternoon traffic pouring out of D.C. in hopes of catching Blackstone at the office.

The thought of confronting the old bastard in his lair to demand an explanation about Saleem and the whacked-out logistics officer was too depressing to contemplate after twenty-four hours of unbroken travel, so he pointed the Escort in the opposite direction and drove the twenty-odd miles to his condo in the lush Virginia countryside south of Alexandria. There'd be time enough on Monday to learn why for the first time in his career he had been given insufficient information on a target.

Besides, he needed the weekend to calm down.

He had committed the unpardonable sin of allowing himself to get rattled.

That was always the first sign.

The condo smelled of stale air and sour milk and he opened the sliding glass doors, peeled off most of his rumpled clothes and settled into a plastic chair on the balcony with a cold beer to enjoy the twilight and sort through his mail.

A soft breeze riffled the trees on the greenbelt below and the sound of childish laughter drifted up from the playground of the nearby middle school. A young couple in gaily colored jogging outfits ran past on the winding bike path and he involuntarily sucked in his gut, thinking vaguely of Diana and wondering, as he always did at such moments, if he had made a mistake by never marrying and having a family, and whether it was too late to consider such things now.

A normal life.

The thought raised a familiar host of nagging doubts about the solitary existence he had chosen for himself and he knocked back the rest of the beer, then, with his mail still clutched in his hand, padded barefoot to the fridge for another beer, discarding the sweepstakes envelopes and final notices warning that his subscriptions to *Newsweek* and *Fortune* were in serious danger of expiring.

The rest of the mail consisted of a few routine bills and a dainty pink envelope addressed to him in his cousin's distinctive flowing script. He tossed the bills and opened Shelly's letter, anticipating the small pleasure of seeing a couple of new family photos and reading a page or two of hometown gossip.

There were no photos in the envelope, which had been postmarked nearly a week earlier, and before he had finished reading the first sheet of embossed stationery he was on his feet and dialing Shelly's number in Bremerton.

He glanced at the answering machine on the kitchen counter as he listened to the ringing on the other end of the line. The machine's flashing light indicated ten messages to be picked up. Strange, because his number was unlisted and, aside from Shelly and a few people at Harvest, he seldom gave it out to anyone.

And everyone at Harvest knew he had been away.

He let Shelly's phone ring for another full minute, then hung up and punched the Play button on the answering machine. His cousin's high, clear voice filled the room.

From the sound of it, she'd been crying.

"Chris," she said, "please call me as soon as you can—" Her voice cracked and it was several seconds before she could continue. "Something awful has happened and you're the only one I can turn to."

The machine beeped, signaling the end of the message. There was a brief pause and Shelly began to speak again.

The second message, recorded twelve hours after the first, was longer. In it she explained that Sonny, her husband of twenty-five years, was missing and that a search was under way for him in a section of forest near the mountain lake where his father's defunct hotel was located.

He listened with growing concern as subsequent messages she had left at two, four, and five days following Sonny's disappearance filled in the sketchy details that she had finally put into the letter.

Two weeks earlier—the day after Kelly had gone undercover in preparation for the South African assignment—Sonny, Shelly, and his two nephews, Mike and Chris (Kelly's namesake), had gone up to the lake for a combined week of fishing at Pop's old spot by the waterfall, and to continue the restoration work they had begun some months earlier on the old lakeside hotel. Shelly, after completing several business courses at the local community college, had

decided that the place possessed distinct possibilities as a bed-and-breakfast inn.

Late on the afternoon of the second day, the
boys had left Sonny casting his fly into the dark
pool beneath the falls high above the lake,
returning to the hotel on their trail bikes to
clean the day's catch for supper. Sonny had
promised to follow along shortly, wanting a few
quiet moments alone in which he hoped to lure
the general, a legendary trout that every fisherman in the Bremerton area had been convinced
for decades lurked beneath a certain rock at the
edge of the fast running water.

Sonny never returned to the hotel.

Kelly felt a sudden chill down his spine,
remembering the logistics officer's warning and
the strange dream he had experienced on the
flight from Zurich, and it occurred to him that
he had never before dreamed of either Pop or
the pool beneath the falls, a place he had last
visited when he was no more than ten years old.
He wondered if the dream had been prophetic,
then shook off the notion, realizing that the
events surrounding Sonny's disappearance had
happened many days before.

On that first day, Shelly and the boys had
begun to search for Sonny shortly after dark,
returning first to the pool where they feared he
might have slipped on the slick, mossy rocks,
hitting his head and drowning in the cold, dark
waters.

That horrible possibility was immediately
ruled out with the discovery that Sonny's trail

bike, a sturdy Honda 500, was no longer parked beside the tree where the boys had last seen it.

Drowned men don't get up and ride away on their trail bikes.

The next logical theory was that Sonny had started back down to the lake, a distance of roughly three miles over a steep although not particularly dangerous trail, and had crashed into one of the numerous stone-filled washes and gullys along the way. The family had begun a meticulous search of the route back to the hotel, spurred by the thought that Sonny might still be lying injured at the bottom of a brush-filled defile, unable either to climb out or call for help.

That search, too, had proved fruitless.

Around midnight, Shelly had sent young Chris to the nearest phone—at a campground on the opposite side of the lake from the hotel—to summon assistance.

At first light on the following day, nearly seventy volunteers from local search and rescue teams fanned out across the mountain to look for Sonny Lasco. By the following weekend, two hundred more searchers, including a troop of Explorer Scouts from Bremerton, a team of bloodhounds from a nearby county, and two National Guard helicopters had joined the search.

Sonny Lasco, for all his bluster, was a much-liked man in the area.

According to Shelly's last message, which had been recorded early the previous day, no trace of Sonny had ever been found. Except for herself, the boys, and a few die-hard friends, the search had been suspended. The local sheriff's office was hinting darkly now at the possibility of foul play. Two convicts had recently gone missing from a forestry crew working in the general vicinity of the lake and it was theorized that they may have killed Sonny for his trail bike and the few dollars in his billfold, secreting his body in one of the hundreds of shallow caves that dotted the rugged mountainside.

"We need you here with us, Chris." Shelly's voice broke at the end of the last message.

Kelly dialed the Lascos' home number in Bremerton again, knowing as he did that no one would answer. Shelly and the boys would still be at the lake, searching on their own for as long as it took. After ten rings he broke the connection, waited for the dial tone, and punched up Blackstone's private number.

The old man answered on the second ring, his mild voice managing to convey a mixture of pleasure and surprise at his favorite reaper's unexpected early return. There could, of course, be no discussion of the African assignment on this or any other phone line.

Not ever.

"Black, I need some time off to attend to a family emergency," Chris said, interrupting his mentor's jolly inquiries about the state of Kelly's health and the weather.

"Why, Chris, of course," he said. "Nothing too serious, I hope."

Kelly quickly outlined the story of Sonny's disappearance as he had pieced it together from Shelly's letter and phone messages, ending with the information that he would be catching the first available flight north.

"Let me arrange that for you while you pack," Blackstone said. "I have a couple of friends in another agency who owe me a little favor."

Kelly didn't know what to say. In the more than twenty years he had been employed by Harvest, he had never asked for anything, had never felt the need to. "I appreciate that very much—" he began.

"Nonsense," Blackstone snorted, brushing away Kelly's halting thanks as though his offer of assistance was too trivial to mention. "Go ahead and get your things together. I'll get back to you within twenty minutes."

Stepping into the bedroom, Kelly stripped off the rest of his clothes and showered with the bathroom door open and one ear cocked for the phone. Toweling himself quickly dry, he dumped the contents of his overnighter onto the bed and rifled the bottom drawers of his dresser for the jeans, wool shirts, and heavy socks he'd bought for an assignment in the Canadian Rockies several years before.

He was digging in the back of his closet for the old green parka he'd liberated from the marines during a brief tour in Alaska when the phone rang.

"Can you be at Andrews in an hour?" asked Blackstone. "There's some transportation leaving for your general neck of the woods. They'll get you close to your destination."

"I'll be there," he answered. "And I really do appreciate this, Mr. Black."

"You just get up there and take care of that family of yours," he replied. "Take as much time as you need." He paused and Kelly was about to ask him who he should see at Andrews Air Force Base when he added, "And, Christopher, don't hesitate to call if we can be of assistance to you. The full resources of the company are at your disposal."

Kelly tried to thank him again, but Blackstone broke off, telling him to get his tail in gear. He had exactly fifty minutes to report to the main gate at Andrews. Someone would be waiting for him there.

CHAPTER 11

Nighthawks

I T was dark by the time he got to the main gate at Andrews Air Force Base where a young lieutenant who looked to be all of fifteen was waiting. After being directed to park the Escort beside the administration building, he was hustled into a jeep for a high-speed ride across the base. They slowed at a gate guarded by a grim air policeman armed with a very nasty-looking machine gun of a type he didn't recognize.

The guard scrutinized the papers the lieutenant flashed at him, then waved them through. The jeep lurched out onto a pitch-dark maze illuminated by blue lights, and careened across the tarmac to a lone hanger on the opposite side of the field. They drove through the main doors of the empty hanger, pulling to a stop before a simple wooden door where another, even younger, lieutenant stood waiting.

"You Kelly?" he inquired around the wad of pink bubble gum in his jaw.

Kelly nodded and was led to a locker room where a grizzled NCO briefly eyed him and began tossing strange items of clothing and equipment in his general direction. When the pile in his arms reached eye level, he was directed to a bench and patiently instructed in the proper donning of the apparatus.

"Looks like you're suiting me up for a ride on the space shuttle," Kelly quipped.

The sergeant exchanged glances with the gum-popping lieutenant, who was casually pulling on an array of equipment similar to Kelly's, but said nothing. He spent a long time adjusting hoses and buckles, then shoved a long printed form at the puzzled outsider, indicating where he should sign. That done, the lieutenant jerked his head in Kelly's direction and led him through a corridor to another door. He opened it and they stepped into the warm night air.

The bird, a matte black contraption comprised entirely of sharp angles, sat waiting on the floodlit ramp. Below its spindly landing gear, half a dozen jumpsuited ground types probed and polished and fussed over it.

"What is it?" Kelly breathed, craning his neck to peer into one of the two giant exhaust cones on the tail.

"Next generation spook stuff," said the gum popper, pointing to a steep aluminum ladder. "Upsy-daisy."

He oversaw the older man's clumsy ascent to the cockpit where another NCO was waiting to strap him into the right seat, a thinly padded bucket that left him free to wriggle his toes and fingers, and little else. "Gees'll snap your fucking arms off like twigs if you ain't careful," commented the NCO, shoving them into contoured grips at the sides of the seat.

The next several minutes were occupied with the NCO attaching tubes to Kelly's suit, affixing a bullet-shaped helmet to his head, then repeating a litany of preflight checks that Gum popper read from a series of glowing computer screens scattered about the cramped cockpit. When they were both satisfied, the NCO withdrew and the knife-shaped canopy whirred shut. Gum popper allowed his passenger a quick grin and a thumbs-up. "You ready to rock 'n'roll?"

Kelly grinned nervously as a deafening blast of sound rocked the aircraft and they thundered out onto the main runway. The bird paused on the tarmac while the kid at the controls mumbled something incoherent into the microphone in his helmet, listened to the tower's reply, and scanned the video arcade before him.

"Ever been in one of these before?" His voice crackled into Kelly's headset, filled with boyish enthusiasm.

Kelly swallowed hard and shook his head.

"Well, hang on to your balls, 'cause you're in for a helluva treat," he said.

"Which way will we be departing?" Kelly asked, trying to make intelligent conversation.

Gum popper grinned and pointed a gloved index finger at the cockpit roof.

Kelly tried another tack. "About how long will we be flying?"

The kid glanced at one of his screens. "Call it eighteen minutes and change."

Kelly was certain he was joking. "To northern Pennsylvania? That means we'll be traveling over fifteen hundred miles per hour!"

"Yeah, well, they said you were in a hurry." The disembodied voice in the tower muttered some more numbers into the kid's radio and he flashed Kelly a toothy smile. "The captain has turned on the no-smoking sign. Please be sure your seat belt is securely fastened."

A thunderous howl filled the cockpit and Kelly was flung back into his seat as the bird leapt down the runway, rotated onto its tail, and screamed straight up into the night sky.

Less than twenty minutes later the black monster roared onto the runway of a remote airbase somewhere near the Canadian border that Kelly hadn't even known existed.

He had figured on renting a car in the nearest town and making his way the rest of the distance to the lake by road. Blackstone's connections, however, had taken the old man at his word. As Kelly stumbled weak-kneed into a locker room nearly identical to the one at

Andrews, another pink-cheeked lieutenant appeared, this one dressed in the familiar green flight suit of regular air force aircrew, sipping a Styrofoam cup of coffee.

"You Kelly?" he asked.

He nodded and while he got out of the space suit and back into his clothes, which the NCO at Andrews had neatly bundled into a small nylon bag, the new looey brought him a cup of coffee and asked where he wanted to go.

"Bremerton, Pennsylvania," he answered hopefully.

The new kid raised his eyebrows. "Bremerton? They told us you wanted to go up in the mountains somewhere."

"Well, yeah," he answered, sipping the scalding coffee. "But I figured since it's dark now and I'm not even exactly sure how to get there from here . . . Well, Bremerton's the closest city."

The young lieutenant jammed a cigar into his mouth and unfolded a standard sectional map on the equipment table. "S'pose you leave the drivin' to us," he said. "Now, just show me where you think you want to get to."

Kelly pointed to the oblong lake outlined in blue on the map thirty miles north of Bremerton. "There's an old resort hotel up there someplace. . . ." He hesitated, trying to remember where Shelly said the hotel was—about three miles from Pop's fishing hole. "It's on the south shore, I think."

The kid glanced casually at the map, then

folded it into his jumpsuit and touched an old-fashioned Zippo to the tip of his cigar. "You got it, pal. Now, just as soon as you finish your coffee we'll saddle up and be on our way."

BOOK TWO

Lake Lazarus

CHAPTER 1

Darkscape

"**THERE** she is, dead ahead!"

The lieutenant at the controls of the nearly silent black attack helicopter pointed to a moonlit strip of water nestled in a long narrow valley between two jagged mountain peaks. He flipped on a tiny red penlight and consulted a notebook attached by a rubber band to his kneeboard.

"'Lazarus Lake,'" he read, "'elevation six thousand, three hundred feet MSL. Five miles long, close to two miles at its widest point. There's one major campground and a few private summer cabins on the northeast shore adjoining the Bremerton National Forest. Most of the surrounding land also belongs to the Forest Service and there are no other buildings to speak of except a large wood frame structure and outbuildings on the south end, formerly called the Summerland Resort Hotel. Hotel closed down for good in 1958.'"

Kelly looked at him in astonishment. "Where in the hell did you get all of that from?"

The kid grinned. "I flew a couple of drug recon missions up here last year," he replied, "checking out the local marijuana crop for the DEA. Those guys make you do your homework."

Kelly looked out over the nose of the chopper. Lake Lazarus grew rapidly in size, filling the windshield with a stark vista of black mountains and sparkling water. He saw a few lights below as they crossed the northern shoreline—the campground, he presumed—and dropped low over the water to skim along the surface near the center of the lake.

They had traversed nearly half its length when the pilot pointed to a single dim light a few degrees to the left of their course. A rambling two-story building with a high peaked roof surmounted by round Victorian turrets at either end took shape on the far shore. As they drew closer he could see that the solitary light he had spotted from the lake was burning in a second-floor window.

"No place on the grounds to put you down," said the kid, flipping a weird night-vision apparatus over his eyes, "but there's a big Forest Service clear-cut about half a mile farther inland that we used for refueling. If I remember right it's just off the access road leading to the old hotel. That be okay?"

"That'll be more than okay," said Kelly. "I can't tell you how much I appreciate this, Lieutenant. . . ."

The kid grinned and put the chopper into a steep turn. "All part of the service," he said.

Two minutes later, Kelly climbed out of the helicopter, stepping stiffly into a stubbled clearing and dragging his belongings out after him. He hurried to the nearby tree line shielding the narrow road from view, then turned and waved, averting his eyes from the rotor wash as the black machine rose a few feet, spun on its own axis, and flew away into the night with an eerie whooshing sound.

When the chopper had disappeared, he picked up the old canvas backpack he had hurriedly packed with his outdoor clothes and surveyed his surroundings.

The moon was still rising and the nearest trees cast long, black shadows into the clearing. An owl hooted somewhere nearby and he started into the trees, wishing he had a flashlight. It occurred to him that this was the first time in years he had entered a rural landscape for some other reason than to track another human being and he let himself relax, grinning at the thought that a snapping twig or a misplaced step here in these peaceful woods wouldn't necessarily result in the usual fatal consequences.

Johnny had parked the truck in the abandoned shed below the road and was making his way up the familiar path to the place where he spent most of his nights.

After leaving the mall earlier, he had stopped at the big combination diner and truck stop near the turnpike where he had consumed a sixteen-ounce T-bone with all the trimmings, then topped it off with a three-tiered banana split and several glasses of orange soda.

Shopping always made him hungry, especially on days like this when he was really just window-shopping—not seriously contemplating taking a girl, but sizing up and evaluating the possibilities, watching the patterns of mall security to see if anything had changed since his last visit, picking a lucky parking spot from which to display his bait; the bait that was now slung over his shoulder in a gunny sack.

It had been a satisfying day and his head was filled with useful information that he felt sure would guarantee the success of his next trip to Penn Center, or the trip after that.

He had just stepped out of the forest and was preparing to climb the steep rocky path leading to the higher elevations when a black shape rose from the trees to his right. The fearful machine swept over him so close that a blast of icy air from its rotors slapped the side of his face. He stumbled and fell headlong to the ground, raising his face from the dirt in time to see the black helicopter flash past overhead and make a sweeping turn toward the lake.

Johnny froze where he was, staring bug-eyed at the disappearing aircraft and trying to decipher what it meant. Had the cops found the man's body after all? Were they searching for him now? Waiting to pounce on him from the shadows of the deep thicket that surrounded his den?

He got to his feet and scrambled back into the safety of the woods. His big fists clenched and unclenched at the sides of his overalls as he stood in the darkness, listening to the familiar cacophony of the forest. His oddly crumpled ears filtered the night sounds of wind in the leaves and of little creatures scurrying through the woods. He cocked his head in the direction of the lake as the sound of a man walking in the brush rose above the natural noises of the mountain.

Reaching into a side pocket of his overalls, Johnny removed the gleaming skinning knife with its yellowing ivory handle and silently flicked it open.

He did not want to kill another man so soon. It was much too dangerous.

Not as dangerous, though, as being caught.

Dropping into a predatory crouch, the razored edge of the skinning knife held away from his body to defend against sudden attack, he moved silently into the trees in pursuit of the elusive footsteps. The predatory stealth and great speed with which he slipped through the black forest was nothing short of amazing, considering his great bulk and seeming clumsiness.

*   *   *

The access road, a rutted strip of crumbling asphalt that looked as if it hadn't been repaired in decades, appeared ahead of Kelly after a few minutes of walking through the forest. Clearing the shadowed tree line, he stepped out into the moonlight and turned in the direction of the lake, walking along briskly and thankful for the opportunity of stretching his legs after having spent close to an hour in the cramped confines of the helicopter. The clear mountain air was cold and refreshing on his face and the fragrant scents of pine and mountain laurel tingled pleasantly in his nostrils.

The twin turrets atop the old hotel building soon came into view above the tops of the trees and he was pleased to see a warm glow of yellow light appear in a small window near the top of the nearest one.

The thought crossed his mind that Shelly or one of the boys had heard the approach of the helicopter, which was silent only in comparison to conventional models, and had gone upstairs to take a look. He quickened his pace, anxious to see his cousin and learn if any progress had been made in the search for Sonny.

As he walked, Kelly reflected on the peace and solitude of the lush green woods that pressed closely in on both sides of the narrow road. Even without having seen the hotel, he could appreciate what had attracted his father to the serenity of this place after a lifetime spent wandering the world in the service of his country.

Kelly allowed himself a moment to regret the

fact that he had never come up here while his father was still alive and filled with enthusiastic plans for restoring the old place, despite the old man's repeated invitations. Those first years, however, right after his return from Nam had been the worst of his life and he had been of little use to anyone, including himself.

Immediately following his release from the marines, he had spent a few desultory weeks at his grandfather's place down in Bremerton—the only place he could think of to go. He had spent his time drinking beer and watching moronic TV shows, seldom leaving the house and reluctant even to look up Shelly and Sonny, terrified of the reaction that seeing the two of them happily married and already starting on their family would stir within his fevered brain. He had wanted only to escape the memories of Diana and Bremerton. He left thinking he might never return.

The road dived into a dark, brooding tunnel of overhanging tree limbs, emerging a hundred yards later onto a sweeping drive that circled around a recently mowed lawn to the gingerbread portico of the hotel entrance.

Kelly stopped at the edge of the lawn to catch his breath and look the old place over, pleasantly surprised at how well preserved it appeared to be. White paint gleamed luminous in the moonlight and he could detect no evidence of the massive dilapidation he had expected to find after so many months of having read the pessimistic descriptions of leaky roofs

and sagging foundations contained in Shelly's
letters.

Hell, the place didn't look half bad, from this
distance at least. He realized that Shelly and
Sonny must have put a tremendous amount of
work into the old building since he had told
them a year earlier that he'd deed them a half
interest in it and the surrounding lakefront property in return for their fixing it up, although he
had made it clear at the time that he would have
been just as happy to have had them sell, splitting the profits with them for all their trouble.

Looking at it now, he could see why they had
decided to go for the renovation. If the inside of
the Summerland Hotel was half as decent as the
exterior, he could easily visualize harried yuppie
couples from nearby New York and Philadelphia
being willing to shell out good money to spend
quiet weekends here.

Maybe Shelly had something with her bed-
and-breakfast idea. It occurred to him that he
could throw in enough cash from his retirement
fund to allow Sonny to quit his job at the
foundry and go to work on the hotel full-time.
God only knew the poor guy had been laid off
more than he'd worked in recent years. . . .

He let the thought die half-formed, suddenly
remembering the reason he was here.

Sonny . . .

The poor bastard had wanted desperately to
join him in the marines. He didn't think his
cousin's husband had ever quite gotten over the
fact that they'd turned him down, for flat feet of

all things. Now he was gone, disappeared without a trace just like . . .

Just like Diana.

The thought hit him like a slap in the face.

Sonny had disappeared just like Diana: laughing and enjoying himself with his friends—or, in this case, his boys—one minute, gone the next.

He reached into the back of his mind to that Christmas Eve more than twenty-five years ago, searching in vain for something solid with which to link the eerie coincidence. Of course there was nothing there.

He shut his eyes, reliving the painful memory.

He and Diana had been dancing for hours beneath the twinkling Christmas lights in the crowded high school gym, pressing their bodies urgently together in time to the sweet, haunting melodies of their favorite records.

The Beatles's "Yesterday" drifted through his mind. He hadn't known it then, but it was to be their last dance together. They'd been wrapped in each other's arms, whispering silly endearments into one another's ears. Hardly dancing at all by that time, just swaying in time to the music.

There had been one magical moment when she had lifted the silver bracelet to the light, twinkling reflections of red and green and blue magically flashing about the bright initials carved into entwined hearts, turning them for the briefest of instants into living symbols of their love. Then her lips were soft upon his, her eyes closing, her honeyed breath against his neck, the silken swell of her hips pressing against his with the unspoken promise of a lifetime's pleasure to come.

The music had finally stopped. Lights coming up suddenly, taking them by surprise, Diana's soft laugh reaching him above the chatter of the other kids on the floor, her hand in his, pulling him back to the table for teasing by their friends.

Shelly and Sonny at the table like a dowdy old married couple, Shelly griping at him to remove the cigarette from behind his ear, a little jealous of Diana because Sonny stubbornly refused to dance . . . Calling it uncool when they all knew it was really his painful self-consciousness that prevented him.

Thoughts unspoken.

He had seen Diana whispering something into Shelly's ear, the two of them laughing as she got up from the table, bending over to peck him lightly on the cheek—their last kiss—and disappearing into the crowd, allegedly to go to the "little girls' room": Strange, he remembered having thought at the time, because girls never went to the girls' room alone. It was a standing joke among the boys. "What do you girls do in there anyway, give each other pointers on how to get rid of hickeys?" Sonny's usual brand of coarse humor drawing a predictable scattering of snickers from the boys and embarrassed giggles from the girls.

Diana disappearing into the festive crowd alone.

Disappearing forever.

They had waited for her to return. Ten minutes. Fifteen.

The lights had dimmed and a new round of songs already begun when Shelly, acting strangely nervous, had gone to find her while he and Sonny sat exchanging worried small talk. Maybe she had gotten sick or something.

More minutes passing. Shelly, too, gone far too long for a quick check of the girls' room.

Chris growing increasingly nervous. Standing at last to go see what was happening and running into Shelly in the center of the crowded dance floor. Snowflakes sparkling in her wind-blown red hair. Nose red, too, from the cold. The beginnings of tears welling up in her eyes.

Something terribly, horribly wrong.

Shelly blurting out an incoherent story. Something about Sonny's car. The sick, cold feeling growing in the pit of his stomach as Sonny, seeming to understand, ran past him: pounding out through the gym doors toward the parking lot as Shelly tried to explain again.

Diana had gone out to the old Ford to get Chris's Christmas present, which Shelly had been keeping for her, and forgotten to bring in from the glove compartment when she and Sonny had arrived at the dance.

"My fault!" She was blubbering incoherently. "All my fault. . . ."

Still confused.

Leaving Shelly standing alone in the center of the dance floor.

Running.

Couples stopping to stare at the commotion.

Running, through echoing, waxy-smelling high school corridors.

Slamming out through the doors.

Outside, Sonny standing helplessly by the old Ford. The passenger door open, the front seat drifted with fresh fallen snow. Footprints around the car indicating some sort of a scuffle. A lone set of tire tracks leading out into the street, mingled with the tracks of a hundred other passing cars . . .

After that . . . nothing.

The local cops standing around asking lots of dumb questions as the tire tracks filled with new snow, certain the kids themselves had something to do with Diana's disappearance. The girl was maybe pregnant? The lovers had maybe had a fight? Did she ever talk about running away? Have another boyfriend maybe? And so on? And so on?

And all the time they were wasting with their stupid insinuations, Diana was being taken farther away from him.

Farther and farther away . . . until there was no chance whatsoever that she would ever be found again.

The final blow had come two days later when Shelly, her eyes red and swollen from too much crying, had appeared at the door to his grandfather's house with the small, gaily wrapped box completely overlooked in all the hysteria.

His Christmas present.

Sonny had found it in the Ford's glove compartment.

It had been three more days before Chris had mustered the courage to open it, as though doing so would sever some final remaining link between the two of them.

He had finally done so, carefully unwrapping the blue-and-silver holiday paper, exposing the simple gold chain with the tiny pendant of a soaring bird in flight. On the back a single word had been engraved.

Forever.

Sonny's disappearance?

Just a coincidence.

Nothing more.

Kelly shook off the hurtful memory and moved up the drive into the shadow of the old hotel, stopping perhaps two hundred feet away.

He raised his eyes to the turret he had spotted above the trees and was rewarded with the sight of a slender female figure silhouetted in the window. She seemed to be looking down across the lawn. He waved but the figure simply turned and disappeared.

The light in the turret slowly dimmed and went out.

Johnny crouched in the deep shadows at the very edge of the moonlit lawn, watching the stranger who stood staring up at the old building. He had slipped silently through the trees paralleling the narrow drive as the man had walked along, patiently stalking the intruder by the sound of his footsteps.

The long skinning knife was damp against his palm as he tried to assess whether or not to kill the stranger. It would be so easy now. The man's back was to him and they were separated by a distance of no more than ten yards. He drew a mental picture of himself leaping from his hiding place, envisioned the man turning in surprise at the sudden rush of footsteps from behind, saw the knife plunging into the stranger's throat, the hot blood spurting.

It was a difficult decision, for, while the stranger posed no immediate threat to Johnny or his girls, the other man—the one he had killed by the waterfall—had also come from the old hotel, territory that Johnny had until recently considered to be part of his exclusive preserve, a place, in fact, where he had always brought his girls for the frequently messy rituals that prepared them to be good. The hotel's large kitchen with its stainless steel sinks and broad countertops had been ideally suited to his purpose.

The first time the other man had come, bringing his family and his racketing motorcycles with him, Johnny had moved into one of the several refuges he maintained in the woods above the lake, anxious to avoid detection at any cost. The move had proved to be a mistake from the start, forcing him to leave his truck in the distant shed and take a long, roundabout route through the forest to reach his hideaway.

He had been relieved that first time, when the intruders had left the hotel after only a few days, fully convinced that things would return to normal again.

Upon his return, however, he had found huge stacks of trash and ruined bedding from the hotel rooms piled on the lawn and shiny brass locks affixed to all the doors.

Undaunted, Johnny had cleverly sprung the new locks and moved back in.

Another mistake!

He had almost been caught the next time the man and his family had unexpectedly returned, and been forced to huddle miserably in the dusty turret above the kitchen for an entire weekend as the sounds of pounding hammers and shouting voices had echoed through the rambling structure.

Afterward, his fear of discovery greater than his attachment to the one place he had always considered secure, Johnny had abandoned the hotel premises.

From that time forward, however, he had spent many long nights pondering ways to displace the intruders without attracting undue attention. Although he had killed the man by the waterfall out of desperation, and not as part of any organized plan to rid himself of the invaders, he had allowed himself to hope that the others would go away as well. He now realized that that had been wishful thinking on his part. The man standing on the moonlit lawn was carrying a bag, and the method of his arrival—by helicopter and without return transportation—made it clear that he, too, intended to stay.

Shifting the knife to his opposite hand and wiping his sweaty palm on the leg of his overalls, Johnny took a fresh grip on the worn ivory handle and calculated the distance to the stranger. He took a deep breath. . . .

A sixth sense born of years of near fanatical adherence to Blackstone's principal that if you thought someone was watching you they probably were raised the hairs on the back of Kelly's neck. He whirled about to face the thick line of trees from which he had just emerged, narrowing his eyes to peer into the shadows.

Nothing moved.

Sweeping up his bag, he backed away toward the hotel, putting more space between himself and the trees. He rapidly scanned the entire circumference of the lawn, moving his eyes in short, jerky arcs across small sections of the terrain in the approved technique taught to him by the marines for night observation, alert for any aberration in the leafy cover, any movement at the peripheral edges of his vision.

Still, nothing moved.

A bird let out a small trilling song among the trees and he smiled at the familiar sound. Breathing a small sigh of relief, he turned and walked across the lawn, detouring around a

defunct fountain and stepping over a fallen
statue. As he walked, he chided himself for
being excessively paranoid, a trait he hoped to
discard once he returned to normal life.

He did not see the dark shadow that detached
itself from the trees at his back and swiftly
melted into the shelter of the black shrubbery
beneath the shadowed wall at the far end of the
hotel.

The Summerland Hotel

T H E covered portico at the front of the hotel sheltered a broad set of brick steps leading to a pair of ornate glass doors. Chris ascended the steps and paused before the doors, turning to look back across the lawn once again. He still had not shaken the vague feeling that there was someone out there watching him.

The lawn was still, as it had been before, its toppled statuary gleaming bone white in the light of the moon. Shrugging off the nagging sensation that he was being observed, he reached for the nearest door and tried it, surprised to find it tightly locked at this early hour. He looked around for a bell and, finding none, looked in through the glass.

Inside, the polished floors of the hotel's spacious lobby were dotted with arrangements of Victorian furniture, velvet sofas and padded chairs grouped in twos and threes about dark tables and fringed floor lamps. To the right side of the room stood a long wooden counter backed by a pigeonholed wall of mail slots. Dark paintings of idealized mountain vistas hung on the paneled walls opposite the desk, surrounding a grand staircase.

The entire space was illuminated by moonlight flooding in through the multiple sets of floor-to-ceiling French doors lining its far end. Beyond the French doors, the sparkling waters of Lake Lazarus shone through from a broad veranda fronting the opposite side of the hotel.

Chris rapped on the door. When no one responded he rapped harder and called out in a loud voice, "Hello? Anybody here?"

A flickering light glimmered against the faded wallpaper at the head of the wide staircase, growing brighter as whoever was carrying it walked along the upper hallway. The light stopped, as though its owner were hesitating before exposing himself to view at the top of the stairs, and he rapped again, the sharp sound of his knuckles on the glass rattling through the still night air. "Hello, down here," he called.

The light moved closer and he pressed his face against the glass, hoping to catch a glimpse of the approaching figure. He drew in a sharp breath and backed away in surprise as a ghostly form glided onto the upper landing and paused to gaze down into the moonlit lobby.

The girl—for she appeared from this distance to be no more than a teenager—stood at the head of the stairs dressed in a nightgown of some thin flowing material that covered her from neck to ankle. Lustrous blond hair curled down about her shoulders, a careless fall sweeping across her forehead to mask her features in shadow. One upraised hand held a heavy silver candelabra, the glow from its five dripping tapers outlining the contours of her full breasts and narrow hips in tantalizing strokes of deep shadow. Her other arm, naked from the shoulder, hung gracefully at her side.

Chris stood frozen at the doors, wondering who she was. She made no further move to descend the stairs. Regaining his composure, he rapped again.

"Who is it?" she called in a tremulous voice.

"My name is Chris Kelly," he called. "I'm a friend of Shelly Lasco. Is she here?"

She shook her head.

"Well, look, can you let me in?" He paused. "I'm supposed to be here. That is," he added clumsily, "Shelly called . . . about Sonny."

She hesitated, then came down the stairs, pausing to set the candelabra on the counter. He caught a quick glimpse of regular features and full lips as she reached over to switch on a shaded lamp above a thick ledger that he assumed was the guest register. She padded barefoot to the door, the moonlight from the opposite end of the lobby silhouetting her body through the thin gown. He could clearly see the outline of the skimpy black panties she wore beneath the sheer material.

"I'm sorry," she said, coming to a stop before him and looking up through the glass of the closed door. "Shelly had to go back to Bremerton to take care of some business. She's probably back home by now."

He nodded. "I see. Well, I'm her cousin. I couldn't reach her at home so I just came straight up here."

She looked at him. Her face was again hidden in the shadows of the darkened room, making it impossible to read her expression.

"So can you let me in?" he asked when she made no move to open the door.

She folded her arms across her chest, suddenly aware of his eyes looking down at her thin nightdress.

"I'm sorry," she finally said. "I mean, Shelly didn't say anyone was coming up tonight. Maybe you should go on down to Bremerton and find her."

Chris was getting irritated. "I can't go down to Bremerton," he snapped. "I don't have a damn car. Didn't you see the helicopter that just dropped me off?"

She shook her head. "I didn't hear anything."

"Dammit, then why were you just up in the turret watching me?"

She looked at him strangely. "I think you'd better come back tomorrow," she said with finality. She pulled the gown tightly about her and turned away.

"Hey, I'm sorry," Chris called. He fumbled in his jeans for his billfold and pulled out a laminated folder. "Look," he called, holding the plastic up against the glass.

She turned back and examined the family photo of Shelly, Sonny, and the boys. "See," he said, pointing to the inscription. "To Chris, from all of us."

"Let me see some ID," she demanded.

He unfolded the laminated accordion, exposing a driver's license and a handful of credit cards. She studied them for a moment, then unlocked the door, stepping away as he scooped up his bag and entered the lobby.

"Thanks," he said, smiling.

She shrugged. "Shelly didn't say anyone else was coming." She looked around the empty lobby. "It appears that everyone has given up on Sonny."

"I tried to call as soon as I heard," he explained as she retraced her steps to the counter. "I was out of the country until this afternoon."

She reached over to retrieve the candelabra and he saw that she was exceptionally pretty, though not nearly as young as he had first imagined.

"Would you like some coffee?" she asked.

He nodded gratefully and she started toward the staircase. He started to follow and she pointed to a dark corridor off to the right. "The kitchen's down that way," she said. "There's a light switch just inside the hallway."

"Oh." The disappointment sounded in his voice. "I had hoped that you might be able to fill me in on the situation up here."

She smiled at him for the first time. "I'd be happy to. In fact, I was going to offer to fix you something to eat, if you're hungry." She looked down at her flimsy gown. "I would feel better with some clothes on, however."

She extended a smooth hand tipped with crimson nails. "By the way, my name is Sherry Mahan," she said.

He took the offered hand, finding it warm and soft. "Chris Kelly," he said.

She nodded and her smile broadened. "You said that before. Why don't you go in and get the coffee started, Chris. You'll find everything out on the kitchen counter. I'll be right back."

He watched admiringly as she turned and started up the stairs, her shapely legs moving gracefully beneath the swirling nightgown.

"Hey," he called, "what's with the candles?"

She stopped at the landing and struck a dramatic pose. "Dramatic, aren't they?" she asked. "I felt like the heroine in a Gothic novel coming down here before." She hefted the heavy candelabra and grinned. "I could claim I was carrying this for protection—I could brain somebody quite handily with it if I had to—but the truth is that there's no electricity above the first floor yet. Sonny is—" Her smile faded and she corrected herself. "He . . . was in the middle of bringing the old wiring up to code before . . ."

Kelly nodded his understanding and watched her disappear down the same upstairs corridor from which she'd first appeared.

*   *   *

Johnny stood in the shadows beside the hotel portico. He had been watching through the glass doors as the man and the woman inside talked, glad now that he had not attacked the stranger out on the lawn. He had not realized that there was anyone else still inside the hotel. Perhaps he might have gotten away with disposing of the man before he ever reached the hotel, but if the woman had seen . . .

Two missing persons would certainly make the authorities suspicious at this point. They would surely start searching the forest in earnest again if two more disappeared.

Johnny had overheard enough of the man's conversation while he still stood outside to understand that he was simply a relative who had come to comfort the widow of the dead man. He didn't seem to be a threat after all.

Contenting himself with the knowledge that the newcomer would probably stay for a day or two and then go away, Johnny silently folded the skinning knife and slipped it into the pocket of his overalls.

He edged away along the side of the building and, from the cover provided by the end of the structure, hurried across the drive and melted back into the thick cover of the trees. Making his way through the forest to the first of the steep paths that would bring him to the security of his den, he let his mind drift back to the pleasant thoughts of the girls he had seen in the Penn Center Mall.

Now that the threat to his safety was really coming to an end, he was anxious to start planning to bring home a brand-new girl.

The sight of the blond woman in the hotel had stirred him and he leaned against a tree, feeling the bad thing beginning to happen deep within his overalls. The bad thing did not scare him anymore, not the way it had a long time ago. He knew how to make it go away.

He fumbled with his buttons, slumping down into the soft, loamy soil against the trunk of the tree and sighing as his thick fingers found their objective. He groaned in pleasure as a burst of golden light flashed in his head and he was seized with a sudden inspiration. It was time to bring home another fair-skinned girl. A beautiful blond, or perhaps a redhead.

He howled his pleasure to the sky as the bad thing exploded upon him and a thick rope of saliva slid from the corner of his mouth to dangle at the end of his triple chin.

He would be extra specially careful with this one.

If she turned out as well as he planned, he would name her Marilyn after his favorite movie star.

Sherry Mahan was thirty-two years old and had been Shelly's best friend for more than five years, ever since she had arrived in Bremerton as a refugee from a failed marriage to a failed actor and the ever-escalating crime and bad air of Los Angeles.

She had rented the small cottage down the block from the Lasco house that had been left to the couple when Shelly's mother had passed away the previous year. Alone and friendless in the small city, which she had chosen for its bright mountain setting and relative safety, she had immediately fallen under the older woman's protective wing, at first becoming Shelly's favorite matchmaking project and, later—after she had finally made it clear that she was in no particular hurry to marry any of the bedraggled bachelors that Shelly and Sonny were always dragging by for her perusal—just a friend.

After having spent the previous weekend assisting in the search for Sonny, Sherry had wangled an early vacation in order to come back up to the lake earlier that day, when it had become depressingly evident that Sonny was not going to be found.

She had spent the afternoon accompanying her distraught friend on one more fruitless foray into the dense woods in search of something that the organized search parties might have missed. By nightfall she had finally talked Shelly into letting Mike and Chris take her back down to Bremerton for a few days of rest and, fearing her friend was near collapse, a medical checkup, by the simple expedient of promising to stay at the lake until they returned, on the off chance that Sonny might somehow show up in need of assistance.

All of the foregoing information she imparted to Chris while firing up the massive coal range in the hotel's drafty kitchen and whipping up a delicious-smelling pair of omelettes that she placed on paper plates while he struggled to keep the toast from burning in the primitive eight-slice toaster.

"So there's still been no sign whatsoever of Sonny?" he asked, fumbling the smoking slices of bread onto a pink paper plate of their own and carrying them to the battered wooden table.

Sherry shook her head sadly. "It's completely baffling," she said, sitting down and buttering a piece of toast. "Generally, the dogs will always manage to turn up something within a few days, especially if there's a body involved." She bit into the toast and continued to talk with her mouth full. "We even managed to get a helicopter equipped with infrared up here on loan from the state troopers last week."

He looked at her quizzically as she began to eat her omelette. "Infrared?"

She nodded. "The heat given off by a human body can be picked up on infrared sensors." She put down her fork and her voice took on a somber tone. "Even a decomposing corpse will show up as differential traces on a really good infrared scanner. The chemical reactions produce heat as the body breaks down," she explained.

"Yeah, I know that," he said, wondering how she happened to have come by that particular piece of relatively specialized knowledge.

"Anyway," Sherry said, returning to her omelette, "everyone involved in the search at an official level seems pretty certain that Sonny is no longer in the area. Otherwise, they reason, the special teams would certainly have turned up some sign of him by now. They've covered this grid in more depth than you're likely to see in most missing-persons searches."

"You seem extremely well-informed about the technical side of this," he said, genuinely impressed by her easy grasp of search-and-rescue techniques, an often complex discipline that he'd seen employed many times by experts in Vietnam.

She shrugged. "I was involved in a few searches in the mountains around L.A.," she said. "Now there's some really rugged terrain for you, right inside the city, too. People get lost and fall off cliffs in Griffith Park all the time."

"Exactly what was it that you did out there?" he asked, his curiosity fully aroused.

"Same thing I do in Bremerton." She grinned. "I was a flatfoot. Actually, an L.A. County sheriff's deputy."

He stared at her. "You're a cop?"

"Detective sergeant." She smiled.

He flushed. "Oh!"

She reached across the table and patted him gently on the arm. "Don't take it too hard," she said. "Beneath this rough exterior I'm really an okay guy."

He began to laugh.

Her smile dissolved. "Do you find the fact that I'm a police officer amusing?" she asked tartly.

He shook his head. "No, it's not that. . . ."

"What then?"

"I was just wondering why you came at me before with a candelabra instead of a loaded gun."

A little smirk lifted the corners of her mouth. "Oh, I had the loaded gun, too."

"No! Where?" he asked in disbelief.

She reached behind her and produced a small automatic from the waistband of her slacks. "Remember those pretty black panties?"

He shook his head helplessly. "Was I staring that obviously?"

She nodded. "I haven't felt eyeballs scanning me like that since I worked vice in West Hollywood."

"Would you consider accepting an apology?" he asked sheepishly.

Sherry grinned mischievously. "For the staring, or for the probable assumption that I was a small-town librarian who reads a lot of detective novels?"

He flushed again. That was almost exactly what he had assumed. "Whatever," he replied.

She nodded and slipped the gun back into the small of her back. "Accepted. Now, suppose we talk about you? You mentioned earlier that you were, what, an international music promoter? Exactly what does that entail?"

"Well, there's not a whole lot to tell," he said evasively. "Mostly I travel around and set up benefit concerts for various charitable organizations."

Sherry looked at him over the rim of her

coffee cup and took a sip. "I see," she said. "And how does that rate you midnight transportation via private military airlift?"

"I'm not sure I understand," he began. "The helicopter I caught a lift on was—"

"A stealth attack chopper," she finished the sentence for him. "We had a couple of them up here last year on a DEA thing. One hundred percent pure spook stuff. So classified the military wouldn't let any of our people get within a hundred yards of them."

"I really don't know what you're talking about," he said with practiced nonchalance.

"Of course you don't." She smiled prettily, lifting a forkful of omelette onto a wedge of toast. "What's more, I'd be extremely disappointed and more than a tad suspicious if you suddenly came clean and admitted outright that you were a spook. You will have to admit, though, that the chopper was a dead giveaway."

"You said you didn't see the helicopter," he countered.

She shook her head. "I said I didn't *hear* the helicopter," she replied. "I happened to be looking out at the lake from the window of my room when it left here going like a bat out of hell, and I got a very good look at it."

"So that was why you went up to the turret." It was a statement, not a question.

She shrugged and bit into her toast.

"Getting back to Sonny," he said, trying to change the subject. "You said the people involved in the official search think he's no longer in the area. But that's not what you think."

Now it was her turn to be evasive. "I have a private theory," she answered.

"But you *do* think you know what happened to him?"

She still didn't answer.

"That's really why you came up here, isn't it," he asked on a sudden hunch, "to check out your own private theory without all those searchers and dogs trampling all over the scenery?"

"You're an extraordinarily perceptive man, Mr. Kelly."

"Chris," he said.

"Chris."

He looked at her expectantly. "So, are you going to let me in on the theory?"

She went to the stove, returned with the stained speckleware coffeepot. She refilled his cup and looked appraisingly at him. "I'd feel much better about telling you if I knew exactly what it is that you do for a living," she said. "I'm asking for a very good reason," she added.

He sipped the scalding liquid, considering the request. Although he had never before been asked to disclose the nature of his work by anyone he might seriously consider telling, the prospectus under which he operated allowed him to disclose the information to other law enforcement officials under certain carefully circumscribed conditions. He decided it was worth stretching the point if there was even a remote chance that it might bring him closer to discovering Sonny's fate.

"Let's say I'm advising you unofficially," he finally said. "Meaning that if you repeat the information I'll deny that I ever told you anything and the very powerful government-sponsored company I work for will probably sue you for libel and ruin your law-enforcement career in the bargain."

"Wow!" she murmured. "Sounds pretty serious." She considered the warning for a moment. "But I still think I need to know."

He nodded solemnly. "I just want you to know what you're letting yourself in for. Did I mention there's also a pretty fair chance we'd both be brought up on assorted charges having to do with national security?" he lied.

She pondered his words for several more seconds. "Okay," she finally said. "Fair enough."

He lowered his voice and leaned forward. "Okay, I kill people who need killing."

Her eyes widened. "Oh, my God! Who? I mean, how? . . ."

"That's all I can say," he warned, "and that was probably more than you wanted to know. I'll just qualify what I've told you by adding that the people I kill are generally international criminals who have somehow managed to put themselves out of the reach of normal law enforcement and that they are very carefully selected and tried in absentia by an international tribunal. Politics are never a factor." He looked at her face, which had gone pale. "I'm sorry if I've upset you."

"It's all right," she replied, taking a large swallow of her coffee. "I mean, it helps me a great deal to know that you're . . . used to dealing with criminals." She thought for a moment longer. "Are you armed now?" she asked.

He reached beneath the table and removed the .38 Chief Special from its ankle holster and set it on the table between them. "And dangerous." He smiled grimly. "Now, let's hear this theory of yours."

She got to her feet and paced to a small window overlooking the lake. "I'm not sure I can verbalize it right now," she said without turning back to face him. "But I've been up to the spot where Sonny supposedly disappeared a couple of times now, including the first day of the search . . . before it got worked over."

"And?"

"And . . ." She turned back to face him. "Something doesn't fit." She shrugged helplessly. "I've viewed a lot of crime scenes and there are certain things you can always spot—signs of a struggle, the victim's belongings. . . . There was nothing like that near the waterfall."

"Leading you to conclude? . . ." He was leaning forward with interest now.

"Either that Sonny left that place before he disappeared, in which case the searchers would have found some trace of him along the single trail leading into the area, or . . ."

Kelly cocked his head. "Or?"

"Or else someone took him by surprise, someone who knew how to sanitize a crime scene."

He stared at her. "You think someone planned to kill Sonny?"

She sighed and leaned against the counter. "I don't know. I mean, that doesn't make any sense, does it?"

He shook his head. "Not that I know of. Sonny always was a hothead, but I never heard of anybody wanting to kill him for it."

"There's another possibility," she said. "He saw something he shouldn't have seen."

"Druggies? You said the DEA had been active up here. The chopper pilot mentioned it, too."

She frowned. "I doubt it. They never found anything up here beyond a couple of marijuana patches. Nothing worth killing for."

"Then what?"

Sherry smiled and spread her arms. "I don't know. That's where I come up blank." She hesitated. "There's just one more thing. That first day, I went up to the falls alone with one of the boys. . . ." She paused again, as though trying to decide whether to go on.

Kelly waited for her to continue.

"Well," she finally said, "it probably sounds silly, but the entire time we were up there I had the strangest feeling that someone was watching us. Not very professional, huh?"

He frowned, remembering the feeling he had had earlier on the hotel lawn, the feeling that some hostile presence was hovering in the darkness, watching him. "Suppose we go up there and look around in the morning?" he said.

*   *   *

Johnny leaned back against the rough bark of the tree trunk and waited for his heart rate to return to normal as it always eventually did after the bad thing had happened. As he waited a tiny spark of doubt began nibbling away at his newfound feeling of safety.

Something far back in the dark recesses of his brain.

Something he had heard the man say back at the hotel.

He pulled his great weight slowly to an upright position and readjusted his overalls. A frown creased the shiny skin of his smooth forehead as he started up the steep path.

As he climbed he became more and more convinced that there was something he needed to remember from a very long time ago.

Something very important.

C H A P T E R   3

Night Games

T H E cold room.

Johnny pulled open the thick insulated door and held the Coleman lantern high, peering into the dark space. A flat, unpleasant odor assaulted his nostrils and he wished he'd remembered to pick up a new vial of peppermint oil. His breath steamed out in a frosty cloud as he stepped into the low-ceilinged room and he was glad he did not have to spend very long in its claustrophobic confines tonight.

Tonight he had merely come to check that all was in readiness for his next girl.

"Hi, Liz. Hi, Farrah." He grinned cheerfully at the two discolored corpses on the low wooden bench at the back of the room, regretting again that he hadn't been able to do more for them. The girls stared back at him, their lifeless eyes glittering in the bright illumination from the hissing pressure lantern and he wondered if they were still mad at him because they hadn't turned out well.

"Cheer up," he whispered, leaning to gently kiss their icy cheeks, careful not to wrinkle his nose at the dead, foul odor clinging to them both.

He touched Farrah's long blond hair, remembering how perfect her rosy complexion had been the first time he saw her. Such a shame about Farrah. The awful massive bruising on her back and buttocks had developed before he had been able to do anything at all about it. He had cried over her at the time. She had been so pretty. Prettier even than Diana. He sniffled now, just thinking about it. He still felt pangs of guilt over having let her down.

He had been almost as unhappy over Liz, not realizing that she had suffocated inside the pickup's long, wooden workbox while he had been stuck in the traffic jam outside of Newark. By the time he had reached the lake many hours later it had been far too late to restore her to anything like herself either.

Johnny had gone ahead and prepared both of them anyway. Farrah had been the first girl he had ever taken from a mall and, like Diana, held great sentimental value for him. Liz . . . well, he just felt so bad about Liz that he hadn't been able to bear the thought of dumping her with his other failures—the ones who'd been badly damaged or died prematurely because they'd fought too hard or been too weak—in the short tunnel that extended into the side of the mountain from the back of the room. The tunnel, which he always hated to enter, was also the repository for all the extra parts: pieces of the girls that were left over after he'd finished making them good.

The very first thing he'd done after Liz's accident was to drill airholes in the carrying box. He had even lined the rough interior with soft woolen blankets so that none of his new girls would suffer as poor Liz had. Johnny had come to the cold room and told her about it right away, too, pointing out how the lining would also protect the girls' delicate skins, hoping to make her feel better. She'd refused to talk to him, though, as had Farrah.

None of the girls in the cold room ever talked to Johnny, but he was as nice as could be to them anyway. After all, it was partly his fault they were here instead of in the comfy family area with Veronica and the others.

Johnny lifted the lantern, plunging Liz and Farrah into darkness. Their eyes shone at him from the shadows as he crossed to the big wooden worktable and hung the light on its hook beneath the shiny tin reflector he'd painstakingly fashioned by hand. The reflector, which had hooks for the two other lanterns he'd need when he actually began a preparation, had thrilled him with its efficiency, directing the powerful white light of the Coleman into a bright circle on the table and, incidentally, shielding his eyes from the glare. He was very proud of the reflector and couldn't wait to try it out.

Before the intruders had come he had had the spacious, well-lighted facilities of the hotel kitchen in which to perform his most delicate work, which he had always performed in the early morning hours by the strong sunlight that came pouring in through the tall windows at that time of day.

His biggest concern upon being forced to move into the dungeonlike confines of the cold room, a space previously reserved exclusively for purposes of storage and concealment, had been whether he would have an adequate light source. As in every other problem he had encountered, his comic books and the TV had provided the solution. He'd gotten the idea for a big overhead light from an old medical show he'd once seen on TV. The concept of fashioning a reflector had come from a recent issue of *Solar Man,* one of his favorite comic book super-heroes.

Reaching beneath the table, he rolled the heavy wooden tool chest to his left side, opening the top drawer and carefully removing the rolled leather packet containing his most prized possession, the set of instruments that, according to his mother, had belonged to his father, and his grandfather before him.

Johnny ran his fingers over the soft yellow leather, enjoying the worn feel of it and deftly untying the cords that held the packet in a roll. Laying the wrap atop the stained chest, he

lovingly unrolled it, exposing the butter-yellow
ivory handles of the precious instruments.
Bright metal gleamed in his rough hands as he
removed the precision-honed saws, the delicately curved blades and periosteal elevators
from their individual pockets, raising each into
the light above the table to examine its cutting
edge, setting them out in order of anticipated
need.

When he was satisfied with the condition and
placement of the instruments, he opened the
next-lower drawer in the chest, repeating his
careful inspection and arrangement of the needles and ligatures and stretchers.

As he worked, Johnny began to whistle a
happy little tune, picturing in his mind's eye
how Marilyn would look lying there on his table,
her golden skin glowing beneath the light of
three Coleman lanterns. The poor thing would
probably be frightened at first, not understanding what was happening to her, whimpering and
pleading with him to set her free.

He smiled to himself, rehearsing the little
speech he would make, setting her fears aside
by explaining about the bad thing. Showing her
just how awful it could be.

She would calm down after that, after he had
made her understand. Perhaps he would even
show her the gleaming instruments, explaining
softly and lovingly how any movement or
attempt to struggle free could cause him to slip
and hurt her very badly, perhaps even ruining
her pretty looks.

They almost always calmed down after he explained.

Chris Kelly stood before the old-fashioned casement window of his second-story room, looking out over the glassy waters of Lake Lazarus. The moon was setting and the thick stands of conifers running down to the water's edge from the surrounding mountains were etched black against the starlit surface of the lake.

He had opened the window after Sherry had let him into the spacious, high-ceilinged room, one of only three that had so far been restored and furnished from the stock of pristine Victorian furniture that Shelly and Sonny had found hidden beneath yellowing dustcovers in the attic. A soft breeze ruffled the white lace curtains framing the window, causing the flame of the single candle on the dresser to waver and dance in the darkened room.

An owl hooted softly from the forest and the clean scent of greenery filled the room as he walked to the four-poster bed and turned down the light coverlet. He sank onto the blessed softness of the mattress, trying to recall how long it had been since he had last slept. The down pillows crept up around his ears as he heard a new sound, from the room adjoining his.

He closed his eyes, listening to the creak of another bed beyond the wall and picturing in his mind the way Sherry Mahan had looked in her filmy nightgown on the stair. Her eyes, blue and searching, dominated the impression and he found a slow smile spreading across his face.

This idealized image of Shelly's best friend surprised and excited him. Although he liked women and had actually been involved in two or three extended relationships in recent years, they had all failed each time he discovered he was beginning to care too much for the other party, frightened at the signs that each of his lovers were beginning to depend upon him, relying on him to protect them from things that were beyond his power. As a result, he seldom thought of women in a romantic sense anymore, avoiding all but the most casual relationships.

Sherry Mahan, however, seemed different from the others he had known. Totally self-possessed and determined to handle whatever situation might arise, he doubted that she had ever leaned on anyone in her life. He smiled at the thought of the compact pistol tucked into the waistband of her black panties and wondered what it would be like to hold her in his arms.

He felt a pleasant flush suffusing his entire body and wondered as his eyelids grew heavy if perhaps he was coming down with something.

Fifteen feet away, in the room next to Chris Kelly's, Sherry Mahan was sitting propped against her pillows, reflecting on the strange man who had turned up at the front doors of the old hotel. She tried to picture him as a professional assassin and failed. Although she wasn't exactly certain what traits a paid killer should possess, nothing she had seen in Chris seemed to fit the profile. Soft-spoken and sensitive, she felt he was somehow miscast for the job.

She wondered if some awful secret drove him.

Shelly had spoken of her world-traveling cousin from time to time, but Sherry couldn't recall her ever having mentioned Chris by name and wondered why. It was evident that her friend had no idea what Chris's actual occupation was and, although she had said that he was unmarried, Sherry had gotten the impression that Shelly's cousin was a much older man; sort of a doughty old bachelor so set in his ways that he wasn't worth considering as a potential match. Strange, given Shelly's avowed mission to find a perfect mate for each and every single person on the planet.

It occurred to her that perhaps he was gay. She immediately dismissed the possibility. No gay man that she had ever met could or would have scrutinized her body the way he had when she had unthinkingly hurried downstairs in her nightgown, not realizing until she had felt his eyes upon her just how revealing the thin material actually was. She blushed at the memory of her earlier indiscretion and tucked her knees up under her, determined to stop mooning like a silly teenager and get back to solving the intriguing little mystery with which she had been amusing herself before Chris's arrival.

Now she pulled the candelabra on her night-stand closer and reopened the lacquered wooden box she had earlier discovered at the back of a kitchen cabinet while searching for matches with which to light the stove. She puzzled over the strange contents of the box, wondering whether Shelly or Sonny knew of them.

Dumping them out onto the coverlet, she held several items up to the warm yellow light, giving each one a cursory examination before dropping it back into the box. As an amateur collector of costume jewelry, she found most of the objects disappointing in that they were either too cheap or too undistinguished to be of any particular interest or value. An explanation suddenly occurred to her and she covered her mouth with her hands.

"Of course," she told herself, "this must have been the hotel's lost-and-found box." She congratulated herself on the cleverness of her deduction, even coming up with an explanation for the preponderance of mundane objects. It was obvious that as time passed and items remained unclaimed, the keepers of the box had simply taken the best and the oldest items for themselves. She tried to remember if Shelly had ever told her what year the hotel had shut its doors. Sometime in the fifties or sixties, she thought. That would be about right.

Sherry yawned and smiled, scooping the remaining contents back into the box. A circlet of blackened silver glinted against the white coverlet and she held it up to the dim light, admiring the cunningly entwined hearts linking the band together. It was a lovely piece and she slipped it onto her own slender wrist, turning it for a better view, but unable to make out the spidery engraving beneath its heavy coat of tarnish.

The bracelet felt somehow right on her and after a moment she reluctantly replaced it in the box. Later, after the shock of Sonny's disappearance had passed, perhaps she would ask Shelly if she might buy the piece. In the meantime, she thought, perhaps she would give it a thorough cleaning.

Leaning over to the night table, she blew out the candles one by one and lay back to gaze up at the shadows on the ceiling. Examining the contents of the box had cleared her mind, something that arranging and cleaning her own collection of costume jewelry always managed to accomplish, and she turned her thoughts back to the strange disappearance of Sonny Lasco. He had had a large motorcycle and a fairly extensive assortment of fishing gear with him. What had happened to those things?

She closed her eyes and tried to picture the waterfall and the deep shimmering pond beneath it—the place where Sonny had last been seen. Something nagged at her, a very obvious thing that must have been overlooked in the search. She tried to remember everything the state trooper had said when he had filled her in on all the steps that had been taken to discover Sonny's whereabouts.

*   *   *

Johnny stared into the tall wardrobe that he had moved into the cold room and converted into a supply cabinet. Something was missing.

He had finished inventorying the contents of the wooden chest a few minutes earlier, satisfied that everything he would need in the way of instrumentation was intact and in its proper place, and had begun checking the other supplies for the upcoming preparation. Nearly all the chemicals and acids and containers were in their proper places. He needed only to obtain the proper body forms and, most importantly, the eyes—although he had several sets of eyes left over from his last visit to the supplier in Trenton, Marilyn would require a special pair: eyes the color of the lake in summer, he had decided. Beautiful eyes.

He looked into the supply cabinet again, trying to decide what was missing. He had had to rearrange all of his supplies after moving them out of their hiding place in the hotel kitchen and he was still not used to the new arrangement. He scanned the packed shelves from top to bottom, counting on his fingers and reciting the inventory to himself.

He halted in midsentence, realizing what was missing. Not supplies at all. Each and every item he would need for his first preparation in the cold room was in its proper place. What was missing was more important.

The lacquered wooden box containing his treasures.

His and his girls'.

Johnny turned his eyes to the rough ceiling of the cold room and howled at his own colossal stupidity. He had remembered everything else: the precious instruments, the massive work-table he had hauled in pieces from the camp-ground on the other side of the lake, the chemicals.

Everything.

Everything except his treasure box.

He sank to the floor of the cold room, clutch-ing his shaved head in his dirty hands and rocked back and forth, moaning. His mother had been right. He was nothing but a big stupid dummy who never did anything right.

He could feel Liz and Farrah watching him from their dark corner. Reflections of the lantern glittered in their glassy eyes. Though he couldn't hear them, Johnny knew they were laughing at him. He covered his ears against the sound that wasn't there.

He was suddenly very frightened.

Chris moaned softly in his sleep and rolled over, clutching one of the soft down pillows to his chest. A light flashed in the silent room and he opened his eyes.

"Hi, honey." Diana smiled at him from the edge of the bed, the heavy candelabra held lightly aloft, the silver bracelet gleaming on her wrist.

"Diana!" He pushed himself up onto his elbow, unable to believe it was really her.

She placed the candelabra on the nightstand

and moved closer to touch his cheek, the filmy material of her nightgown rustling seductively in the still air. "I missed you so much, Chris." A golden tear glistened on her cheek and he reached out to touch her, feeling the wetness on his hand.

"Honey, I couldn't find you," he whispered. "I tried and tried. . . ."

She pressed herself to him, the swell of her breast warm against his naked chest, her hot breath upon his neck. "It wasn't your fault, Chris," she whispered. "You couldn't have known!"

He felt a tight ache in his throat and hot tears welling up in his eyes. "Oh, Diana . . ."

"Don't let him get away with it, Chris!"

He caressed her smooth shoulder, felt the electricity of her fingertips brushing along his leg, awakening long-forgotten sensations of urgent couplings in the front seat of his dad's old Buick. "Who, honey?" Moaning, only half listening to her words.

"Him," she said, her voice filling with hatred, "the one who took Sonny away."

He looked down at her in confusion, golden tresses splayed across his sweating arm. "Sonny?"

She pulled away from him, the candelabra suddenly in her hand again. Growing brighter. "Don't let him get away with it, Chris!" Her face now a hard mask.

"Diana!"

The candles blazed, the glare burning painfully

into his eyes. He shielded his face with his hands.

"Diana, wait!"

Hot light, burning his cheek and forehead. He squinted into the blaze trying to see. . . .

A bird chirped somewhere outside the open window. A hot shaft of morning sunlight pouring onto his face.

He sat up, blinking.

Shook his head.

"Christ!"

C H A P T E R   4

The Waterfall

K E L L Y showered in a circle of garishly flowered plastic hung above a claw-footed tub in the old-fashioned bathroom at the end of the hall, having first noticed the already damp mat beside the tub and the rumpled towel on the rack beside his own. Sherry was obviously up and about early.

Standing before the stained mirror with his razor in his hand, he tried to remember the strange erotic dream, saw Diana's face clearly in his mind's eye: something he hadn't been able to manage for years.

As a reaper, he firmly did not believe in dreams, much less ghosts.

Still, he reflected, the dream had touched him. He wondered if the fact that his subconscious had projected Diana's face onto Sherry—flowing nightgown, candelabra and all—meant something. A smile flickered across his lathered face. Sherry, too, wanted to find Sonny, thought also that someone had waylaid him. . . .

The smile faded as he remembered the other dream he had had: Muktar Saleem and Pop at the waterfall. Two dreams in two days. Then there had been the other, more disturbing, incident at Mabula. For a moment he had actually allowed himself to believe that his deadly shot had failed to kill Saleem.

What in the hell was going on inside his head?

He finished shaving and splashed cold water onto his face, afraid that he knew exactly what was going on. He had seen it before, in reapers ten years his junior, reapers who now manned desks in the Arlington supply center and whose coffee cups trembled in their hands at odd moments. You just couldn't go around subjecting yourself to the stresses of killing people, no matter how righteously, indefinitely.

Blackstone's words.

One day, according to the old man, it all caught up with you. If you were lucky you got off with a permanent case of the shakes. If you weren't so lucky . . . Kelly vividly recalled a reaper named Collins. One afternoon just before lunch, he'd become absolutely convinced that St. Francis had appeared on the monitor of his computer while he was typing out an ordnance requisition for an upcoming assignment. Fortunately, a secretary had overheard Collins discussing his marching orders with the good saint *before* he'd taken the twenty kilos of high explosives on his requisition and wiped out the headquarters of a major paper company whose logging activities were rumored to be threatening the habitat of a rare variety of flying squirrel.

Kelly stared into the mirror, holding up his hand to see if it trembled.

Not yet, thank God.

He only imagined the dead coming back to life.

He found Sherry on the broad veranda overlooking the lake. In her faded jeans and old UCLA sweatshirt she looked like a teenager sitting there in one of the old painted rockers, sipping her coffee and nibbling toast from a buttered stack of slices on a small tray perched atop a spindly plant stand.

"Hi," he said, helping himself to coffee from a dented silverplate service on the tray and spreading a thin layer of grape jelly on a piece of toast.

"Beautiful, isn't it?" she asked, gazing out over the lake.

He walked to the railing of the veranda and looked out over the lake. A slight haze still lingered over the dark water and a couple of fishing boats bobbed on the surface far out toward the center. "My grandfather used to bring me up here when I was just a kid," he said. "When I was about six, I had a picture book of the Atlantic Ocean and the first time we came up I was pretty sure that this was it."

"Did you stay here, at the hotel?"

He shook his head, laughing. "Pop was more the tent and sleeping-bag type," he replied. "We used to camp out up by the falls."

Her features brightened. "Then you must know that area pretty well."

"'Fraid not," he confessed. "I couldn't have been more than ten or eleven the last time I was up there. About all I really remember was that it was a long walk for a little kid and that it's noisier than hell right around the waterfall itself. We used to shout at each other to make ourselves heard."

Sherry nodded, remembering her own visits to the falls. Mike had had to shout at her to explain where he'd last seen Sonny's motorcycle. That started a chain reaction in her head, something that often happened when she was working on a case. Someone might have slipped up on Sonny using the noise from the waterfall as cover. . . .

". . . I said when do you think we should get going?"

She turned to see Chris looking at her. Smiled. "I'm sorry, I'm afraid my mind was someplace else. I thought maybe we'd go up to the waterfall first thing. The boys left their trail bikes here so it shouldn't take us more than twenty minutes or so. Afterward, we can ride around the lake to the campground. I need a few supplies and there's a phone." She hesitated. "I presume you're anxious to call Shelly and get down to Bremerton."

Chris frowned and slowly shook his head. "I'm not in any particular hurry to get to town," he said. "If there's anything to be learned up here that might put us onto Sonny's whereabouts, I'd prefer to be on hand, and I think that's what Shelly would want." He crossed to the breakfast tray and snatched up another piece of toast. "Also, I guess she probably told you that Bremerton doesn't hold any fond memories for me," he added.

Sherry looked at him, puzzled. "I'm not sure I know what you mean."

He smiled ruefully, sorry he'd raised the subject. "Then forget I mentioned it," he said. "It's an old wound from years back. One of the reasons I hate going back to Bremerton is that everybody else still remembers." He saw her expression and laughed. "There, now I've got your brain racing in high gear trying to figure out what in the hell I'm talking about."

She tilted her head, waiting for him to go on.

He spread a layer of jelly on the toast and sighed. "I'm sorry," he said, "I wasn't trying to sound mysterious. It's just that when I was in high school my . . . girlfriend was kidnapped from a Christmas dance, and presumably murdered. It made the papers all over the East Coast at the time and was the only kidnapping Bremerton ever had." He shrugged helplessly and set the toast back on its tray. "People mean well," he said, "but it seemed like no one in town could see me after that without remembering." He winced, recalling painful encounters he'd suffered on the streets years later, even after Nam.

"They just couldn't let it go," he explained, "always having to tell me how sorry they were and that I shouldn't blame myself for what happened—" He broke off, gazing at the distant line of trees on the far shore.

"And did you?" Sherry was gazing up into his eyes.

"What, blame myself? You're damn right I did. For years and years afterward. I should have been keeping an eye on her." He turned away, pacing to the railing and staring out over the lake. "Oh, hell, what's the use? I mean, even when you know there's nothing you could have done, you still feel that guilt. You carry it around with you every day of your life."

He turned, surprised to feel her touch on his shoulder. She was standing beside him, smiling.

"Were you very much in love with her?"

His frown dissolved and he shook his head. "Hell, I don't even know anymore. I was seventeen years old. When you're that age, the other person seems perfect. Maybe we would have fallen out of love the next month. Maybe we would have gone on and gotten married and had six kids. . . . I just wish I could have done *something,* you know?"

She nodded and handed him his toast. "Maybe we can still do something about Sonny," she said.

He took the toast from her and smiled. "Thanks."

*   *   *

The trail bikes, a pair of well-used Honda 250s were parked beside Sherry's Mustang convertible in a small hotel outbuilding sheltered by the trees at the edge of the lake. Chris looked them over, checking the tanks for gas and familiarizing himself with the controls. "You ever ridden one of these?" he asked.

"They give them to twelve-year-olds, don't they?" She smiled gamely and straddled the nearest bike. "Just show me how to start it."

"Not so fast." He laughed. "There are a few things you need to know first. He climbed on the other bike and gripped the handlebars. "Look," he said, pointing to various controls, "clutch, hand brake, throttle . . ."

Sherry examined her own bike, touching each item as he mentioned it.

"Okay," he said, raising his foot off the ground. "Down here on the side of the engine you have your gearshift. That little pedal on the other side is the foot brake. Rule number one is that whenever you need to stop or slow down you always apply the foot brake first. Got it?"

She grinned, pressing on the tiny pedal with her toe.

"Good, now repeat it."

She stared at him, offended. "Excuse me?"

His eyes sparkled. "Repeat what I just said."

She rolled her eyes. "Whenever you need to stop or slow down, always apply the foot brake first," she repeated in a singsong, let's-get-on-with-it voice.

"Good. Because if you hit the hand brake first—that's the one connected to the front wheel—you're liable to end up on your head."

He stood over the bike, raising his foot to a metal lever jutting from the side of the engine. "Okay, this is the kick starter. You might want to cover your ears because this thing is going to make a hell of a racket when I start it up in here. . . ."

"Wait," she said, "don't start it!"

He paused with his foot poised above the starter. "Something I forgot to mention?"

Sherry climbed off her bike and paced to the open door, raising her eyes to the wooded mountain slope rising majestically behind the hotel. "No," she said. "But if there is someone up there—someone who did something to Sonny—they're probably assuming the search is over by now."

"Damn, you're right!" He jumped off his bike and joined her in the shadowed doorway. "So why announce that we're coming up for another look by blasting up the hill on two of the noisiest contraptions known to mankind?" He looked at her with newfound respect. "I should have thought of that myself."

"Why," she asked contentiously, "because you're the man?"

He shook his head. "No, because I'm supposed to be the spook. Hell, if I made a dumb mistake like that in the field I'd be dead."

"Come on," she said, taking his hand. "It's a long walk."

He allowed her to lead him out into the sunshine, wondering if he really was beginning to lose it.

They heard the noise of the waterfall five minutes before they saw it, stepping out of the shady woods and onto a sunlit notch cut into the side of the mountain. They had been climbing for more than an hour and both their faces were bathed in a glistening sheen of perspiration.

"It's just on the other side of that big hump." Sherry pointed to a large dome of granite protruding from the bottom of another wooded slope above them.

Chris scanned the surrounding terrain, trying to recall the last time he'd been up here with Pop. The lake glittered in the late morning sunshine a thousand feet below. He remembered the breathtaking view clearly. Nothing else seemed familiar. "Okay," he said. "Why don't we just hike up there nice and easy just like a couple of tourists. If there's anybody around, we'll let them come to us." He felt beneath his sweater for the .38 tucked into his belt. "Got your gun handy?"

She nodded and together they proceeded up the rocky path, rounding the outcropping of gray stone. The sound of the falls was much louder here. He took her hand in his and squeezed. They stepped through a screen of mountain laurel and onto a smooth, sunny plateau split by a cascading brook. Just ahead, framed by a pair of mature pines, lay the pool that fed the brook. The falls towered fifty feet overhead, wreathed in a cloud of mist shot through with the colors of a permanent rainbow.

The noise was deafening.

Chris stared into the falls, remembering the vivid dream he had experience on the plane, the dead men appearing through the shining veil of water. He forced the memory from his mind, scanned the clearing and the overhanging mountainside instead, his eyes critically assessing the tangled growth of brush and flowering trees sprouting from a series of high ledges flanking the falls on either side.

The nearly vertical slope offered at least a dozen points where an observer could remain hidden from below. Making do with the knowledge that no one could reasonably have been expected to have heard their approach, he exchanged a glance with Sherry and they walked to the edge of the pool. "Let's just sit down and go over what we know," he said, leaning close to speak directly in her ear.

They found a warm boulder a few feet from the water and sat, leaning against each other like a pair of honeymooners.

"When the boys left Sonny he was standing right over there, casting for trout." She pointed her chin in the direction of a flat rock projecting a few feet into the pool from the stony bank.

Kelly followed her gaze, noting that the rock was less than twenty feet distant from the falls, as close as you could get without getting drenched by the spray. A man standing there, his back to the clearing, would be completely deaf to an approach from the rear. As an assassin, he could not imagine a more perfect killing ground. But why sneak up on a man and kill him if all he was doing was fishing? Sonny must have seen something.

He got to his feet and went to stand on the flat rock. Ahead he had a view of rippling water backed by a towering pile of rubble and broken tree trunks that appeared to be the remains of an old avalanche. He turned and looked behind him. This view was more promising. Across the clearing the path emerged from behind the granite dome. He envisioned someone rounding the blind corner and spotting the lone fisherman staring at him from the rock.

Higher up, a number of dark shadows hinted at caves or depressions among the rocks. A hiding place? But for what? It still didn't make any sense. He returned to the boulder where Sherry was still sitting engrossed in thought.

"What about the motorcycle?" he asked.

She looked up, startled. "Over there by the first tree," she answered. "Mike said the kickstand was broken so Sonny leaned it against the trunk."

Kelly nodded and sauntered over to the tree, a huge pine five feet around at the base. He stood staring at it for some seconds, seeing rough bark and the dark outline of what could have been an oil stain on the ground. He turned back to see Sherry kneeling at the edge of the rippling water, trailing her fingers in the icy pool.

"Nothing there," he said when he had crossed the clearing and knelt beside her.

She looked up at him with shining eyes. "Something has been bothering me about this place from the very beginning," she said excitedly, "but I haven't been able to put my finger on it. It just hit me a minute ago."

He waited for her to go on, raising his eyes to the surrounding cliffs. If there were someone up there watching them now, they were perfect targets.

"I'm listening."

"Remember when I told you that I'd been on a lot of crime scenes but I'd never seen one that struck me quite like this before?"

"Yes?"

"Well, that's because it *wasn't* a crime scene. Not really. I mean, the people who came up here looking for Sonny were searching for a missing fisherman, not a hidden body. Once they'd established the fact that his bike was gone, they assumed he must have taken it somewhere else and scratched this place off their list."

He frowned at her, his mind trying to catch up with hers. "Yeah?"

"The pool," she breathed in a hoarse whisper, casting her eyes into the dark, rippling water. "No one ever bothered to search the pool."

"Oh, Christ!" he breathed.

"He could be down there. . . ." she said.

He completed the chilling thought for her. ". . . along with the missing motorcycle and his fishing gear."

Sherry started to her feet. "We've got to get a forensic team up here right away. Divers—"

Kelly grabbed her arm, pulling her back down to his side. "Not just yet," he said.

Fire sparked in her eyes. "What? Why in the hell not? Sonny's body could be right below us."

"And suppose it is?" he asked. "What then?"

"Why, then we'd know—"

"Only what we already suspect anyway," he said. "Meanwhile, we'd have filled this place up with cops and divers, and whoever killed Sonny—somebody who's probably just starting to feel safe about now—would be fifty miles away before we got the body down the hill . . . assuming there even is a body."

"What do you suggest we do?" It was more a challenge than a question.

He trailed his hand in the chilly water. "I don't know," he said. "How do you feel about skinny-dipping?"

She stared at him, trying to gauge whether he was really serious. It occurred to him that this was the first time he had actually gotten the better of her.

Tracy Swanson was cute, and she knew it.

Tooling along the short strip of interstate

highway connecting her wealthy Philadelphia Main Line neighborhood with the sprawling industrial suburb of Fort Washington, she could feel the eyes of the other motorists on her. And why shouldn't they stare? Everything about Tracy, from the red BMW convertible her bewildered father had given her on her sixteenth birthday to the gorgeous tangle of curly blond hair whipping about her pretty face, said Look at me, I'm special.

She had just finished talking to Daisy Vandeveer, her very best friend in the whole world, and one of *the* Vandeveers, on the miniature cellular phone—another gift from her father—that she kept tucked in her Gucci bag. She was on her way to the Penn Center Mall for an afternoon of shopping. It wasn't that she needed anything, in fact, shopping bored her to death, but her stepmother, Trish, had yelled at her this morning about borrowing her idiotic Chanel handbag without asking, and she was out for revenge. Tracy always got revenge, usually by putting a further strain on the Gold Card that her father didn't have the guts to take away from her.

Just the thought of that bitch her father had married after her mom had died made her hate him all the more for his weakness and she wondered how much she could actually spend in one afternoon if she really set her mind to it.

Spotting the Penn Center exit directly ahead, she whipped the steering wheel violently to the right, cutting off three lanes of traffic and earning a blast from the air horn affixed to the top of a huge eighteen-wheel truck. She flipped her middle finger at the enraged driver, and the red car roared down the exit ramp thirty miles an hour faster than the posted speed limit. She just hoped she got another ticket so her father could pay for that, too.

She brought her car to the briefest of stops at the bottom of the ramp, rocketing out into the traffic of the busy boulevard fronting the mall. She drove half a block farther, swerved to avoid a frightened-looking woman in a Cadillac, and screeched down the steep incline leading into the Penn Center's underground parking garage.

Tracy was already pissed as she guided the BMW through the cool, subterranean tunnel of the garage and the fact that the first two levels she passed had flashing Full signs posted at their entrances did nothing to improve her mood. If she missed Daisy and had to shop alone she was really going to be—

SKREEEEEK!

She slammed her foot onto the brake pedal as an ancient rattletrap truck loomed ahead of the BMW and lurched to a stop, filling the narrow aisle she was speeding into. The red car slewed to a halt on the slick concrete floor and she found herself staring at an expanse of rusting black metal with the single faded word lettered in a half circle about the antlered head of a crudely painted deer: TAXIDERMY.

Tracy raised her sparkling blue eyes from the door of the truck and found herself looking directly into the face of an obscenely fat man in grimy overalls. The fat man leered at her, revealing a mouthful of crooked yellow teeth. He ground the starter motor and the truck's stalled engine sputtered to life again.

"Get out of my way, you fat, fucking pig!" Tracy screamed at him and leaned on the horn button. The sound blasted through the enclosed garage, startling her with its intensity and she released the button after a moment.

The fat man grinned at her and raised a thick dirty finger, which he waggled in front of his bulbous nose. "Y-you're a . . . b-bad girl!" he stammered in what seemed to be an amused tone. "B-bad girl!"

Tracy's mouth dropped open and a sudden unreasoning chill convulsed her tanned young body as the fat man gunned his engine and the old truck lurched off into the depths of the garage.

Another car blew its horn behind her, making her jump, and she twisted around in her seat to see a middle-aged man in a blue Chevy motioning for her to move on. "Fuck you!" she screamed, jamming the car into gear and driving down onto the same dark lower level the rattletrap truck had entered. At least it would be easy to find a space down there, she thought, the incident with the fat man already fading from her mind.

She just knew she was going to be late for her meeting with Daisy Vandeveer.

*   *   *

The water was incredibly cold.

Chris Kelly had been in the pool for less than two minutes and already he could feel the numbness attacking his extremities. He was on his second dive and so far he had encountered nothing in the murky depths but a few good-sized trout that had stared at him before darting easily out of his path.

He pushed up toward the surface, slowing his ascent momentarily in order to admire the view of Sherry Mahan's extraordinarily long legs and nicely rounded bottom. Too bad they weren't really skinny-dipping, he mused, half tempted to snap the elastic on her panties.

"God, I am freezing!" She uttered the words through chattering teeth as he broke the surface beside her. Although she had been treading water at the edge of the pool, her hand within easy reach of the small pistol concealed beneath the pile of dry clothing on the bank, her hair had somehow gotten wet and it clung to her face in attractive ringlets.

"Why don't you get out and dry off?" he gasped over the roar of the falls. "I don't think he's down there."

She pulled herself up onto the flat rock where Sonny had last been seen and sat shivering in the warm sunlight. "Are you sure?" she called.

"Hell, no, I'm not sure," he yelled back, "but it's not a very big pool and I've looked under all the ledges where you might be able to hide a body."

She extended a trembling hand to him. "Come on and get out, then, before you get frostbite."

He nodded. "In a minute. There's one place left to look." He turned his head toward the falls.

She followed his gaze to the thundering water. "I don't think you should go in there," she said.

He grimaced and took a deep breath, doubling over and kicking his feet into the air.

The water beneath the falls smashed against him as he pulled himself hand over hand across the boulder-strewn bottom. Visibility was virtually nonexistent here and he peered in vain into recesses beneath several boulders, confirming with his hands that they hid nothing more than smaller boulders. He propelled himself forward again and the water suddenly quieted as he swam into a dark void. Looking up at the sun-speckled surface, he realized that he was beneath an overhanging shelf of rock behind the falls.

His lungs were beginning to burn as he forced himself deeper into the natural cave that had been formed by eons of swirling water and he strained to see what was ahead.

Nothing.

He was on the point of turning back, painfully aware that he would have to backtrack beyond the shelf before kicking to the surface or risk smashing his head on the overhanging rock.

His chest was aching for another breath when his hand touched something smooth and cold and hard. He whirled about, grasping the thing in the water, and brought his face up to it. A stray beam of reflected sunlight shone past his

shuddering body and something gruesomely soft
and flapping brushed across his lips.

Chris Kelly screamed in the freezing darkness.

CHAPTER 5

Snare

WAITING.

Johnny sat in the cab of the old pickup, waiting.

As he waited, he munched Twinkies from the small box he kept in the glove compartment for emergencies.

Johnny loved Twinkies. He liked the sound of the crinkly cellophane wrappers as they tore, releasing the soft pasty odor, and the first taste of spongy yellow cake in his mouth as he bit off the end of each succulent pastry and inserted his long red tongue into the smooth, sweet tunnel of creamy filling. Curling his tongue and sucking the filling out of the cakes made him feel like Dracula.

He crammed the remains of his second Twinkie into his mouth and grinned into the rusted side mirror bolted to the door of the truck, half hoping to see glistening fangs growing out of his pink gums. His crooked yellow teeth gleamed dully back at him and he shrugged. Hoping for fangs was really too much.

He shifted his head away from the mirror, focusing his gaze on the chrome-lined doorway leading to the mall escalators. He had been waiting for more than two hours for Marilyn to return.

Johnny did not mind waiting. At such times he thought of himself as a powerful mountain lion, able to sit motionless for hours while his unsuspecting prey moved ever closer, unaware until the instant he pounced that she was even being hunted.

He liked that.

Turning his gaze away from the mirror, he glanced down at the red convertible parked beside the truck. He had waited almost an hour for the space next to it to open up, sitting patiently in a dark corner at the end of the long aisle of cars on the third level of the garage, watching.

His patience had finally been rewarded when a battered Camaro filled with yelling high school kids had left the mall and he had guided the pickup into the coveted spot.

All that remained now was for Marilyn to return from her shopping trip.

Johnny closed his eyes, noisily sucking the remains of the Twinkie from between his teeth and picturing how Marilyn had looked as she had jumped from the red car and hurried to the escalators, her red high-heeled shoes clicking against the concrete, smooth buttocks shaking in perfect rhythm beneath the silky fabric of her short black skirt.

He was glad she had been so mean to him earlier, her outburst on the parking ramp showing him just how bad she was; how much she needed him to make her good again.

Johnny smiled contentedly as he felt the bad thing stirring within his overalls. He knew that taking Marilyn was right, more right than any of the others he had ever taken. He had known it from the moment the truck stalled on the parking ramp and he had looked up at the blast of the horn from the shiny convertible to see her glaring at him with her perfect blue eyes, her pouty red lips forming bad words to curse him.

Even though he had not come to the mall to take a girl today, but only to examine the parking garage one more time, he knew that he would never find another girl as blond and beautiful or as bad as Marilyn.

He frowned, trying to remember all the things he still had to do before he would be able to make her good, things he had planned to take care of over the next few days. There were chemicals to buy, and fuel for the lanterns, and the eyes, beautiful blue eyes the exact shade of the water in Lake Lazarus.

The eyes were always the hardest thing. Animal eyes, the kind you could order from the taxidermy supply catalogs, weren't right. You had to have human eyes, and there was only one place to get them.

He prayed to his mother and the golden star that Marilyn would keep long enough for him to get everything he would need.

He wanted her to be perfect.

Johnny looked into the back of the truck, at the big wooden box bolted securely across the metal bed, glad that he had stopped to pick up a fresh supply of girl bait just before coming to the mall. Without it, he doubted he would be able to lure her to him.

"I can't believe you want to just leave him down there!" Sherry was angrily pacing up and down on the veranda, her damp hair clinging to the neck of her sweatshirt. "How can you even consider such a thing?"

Kelly sat in one of the rockers. There was a blanket wrapped around his shoulders and he was sipping the warmed over remains of the breakfast coffee. Even though they had returned to the hotel more than an hour ago, following a hurried descent through the midday heat of the forest, he was still chilled to the bone.

He closed his eyes, trying to decide whether his inability to warm up was due to the time he had spent in the frigid waters of the pool or the memory of the hideous sight that had confronted him in the shallow cave behind the waterfall: Sonny Lasco, his hands and legs bound securely to the frame of the motorcycle with fishing line, his dead eyes staring straight ahead as a huge rainbow trout calmly nibbled at the ragged strands of brain tissue bulging from the top of his skull. . . .

He opened his eyes and looked up at Sherry. She was standing over him, hands planted firmly on her hips, awaiting his reply.

"Think about it," he said, keeping his voice as calm and even as possible. "Whoever put Sonny down there went to an amazing amount of trouble."

They had closely examined the area behind the falls following his grisly find, discovering deep scratches in the rocks where the heavy motorcycle had been dragged up to the edge, scratches that had then been cleverly disguised beneath a layer of fresh dirt. Nearby, they had found a shallow hole where the bike's fuel and oil had been dumped and buried, probably to prevent it from leaking out into the pool where it would form a suspicious slick on the surface. Kelly was willing to bet that when the bike was finally recovered they would find the gas tank and crankcase packed with dirt. They had discussed all of this on the way down the mountain.

Sherry shook her head. "Of course they went to a lot of trouble, they'd just murdered a man."

"But you've got to ask yourself why," he insisted. "Why go to that much trouble to hide a body when you could just drag it into the brush and be miles away before anyone discovered it?"

"All right," she said, "so the murderer is still up there, or in the vicinity anyway. All the more reason to bring in the authorities."

He shook his head, exasperated. "We've been all over this before. It's more than his just being in the vicinity. There's something around those falls that draws him back. Something so important to him that he had no alternative but to conceal the body so well that no one could reasonably be expected to find it. Don't you see?"

"No," she said. "I don't see."

"He's going to go back there again," said Kelly. "He's *got* to go back . . . as long as we don't scare him off."

She leaned against the railing and folded her arms across her chest. "What are you suggesting?" she asked suspiciously. "Do you want to set him up like one of your assassination targets and kill him?"

The stinging note of sarcasm in her voice made him wince. "Of course not," he answered evenly. "But before we flush him out and run the risk of losing him I would like to try to find out who he is and, if possible, what he's hiding up there." He paused, adding in a softer voice, "There's nothing we can do for Sonny now, except maybe to help catch this guy."

Sherry furrowed her brow. What Chris was suggesting went against all of her training as a law enforcement officer. At a deeper level, however, she knew that he was probably right. As long as the killer felt safe he would in all probability feel confident in returning to the falls

whenever he felt the need. The noise and commotion of even the most discreet police investi-
gation would certainly involve removing the
body from the pool, a task that simply could not
be accomplished in secret. After that, the killer
would simply shun the place forevermore, even
if he remained in the area.

"Let's assume I go along with your idea," she
said, hastening to add, "and I'm not making any
promises. How would you proceed?"

"Okay," said Chris, standing and shrugging off
the blanket. "Chances are very good that the
killer is a lifelong resident of the area. The fact
that he knew there was an underwater cave
behind the falls probably means he knows these
woods like the back of his hand. So let's assume
he lives up here or, at the very least, spends
most of his time up here. How many people do
you think fall into that category?"

Sherry shook her head. "I don't know, probably no more than a handful. I'd guess there are a
dozen or so Forest Service personnel, then
there are the people who run the campground
at the other end of the lake and maybe a few
families living year round in cabins."

"So we begin by finding out who they all are,"
he said, "preferably without raising any undue
suspicion."

"I can probably get most of that information
down at the county courthouse in Bremerton,"
she said, her eyes flashing at the prospect.
"Damn!" she exclaimed, suddenly remembering
what day it was. "Today is only Saturday. I'm not

going to be able to get in there to look at the records until Monday."

"That's okay," he said. "I think we should probably spend the rest of today and tomorrow poking around up here anyway. Maybe we can get a lead on what our man is protecting. I'd also like to get a look at that campground. Since that's where most of the people seem to be, we might just pick up some local gossip that will give us a clue. Whoever the killer is, he's got to be one big sucker in order to have manhandled that motorcycle into the pool the way he did."

"Or two medium-sized suckers," Sherry said.

"Or three muscular midgets." He laughed.

She found herself laughing along with him and realized she had bought into his scheme, hook, line, and sinker. Her laughter faded as she remembered that they were talking about Sonny's murderer, or murderers. "What are we going to tell Shelly?" she suddenly asked. "I mean, shouldn't she at least know that Sonny is . . . dead?"

Kelly averted his eyes. "What do you think?" he asked.

Sherry nodded silently. There was no way they could tell Shelly, or anyone else. Besides, she reasoned, telling Shelly they were leaving Sonny where they found him would be just too cruel. It was going to be hard enough explaining it afterward.

She crossed the veranda to Kelly and put her hand on his shoulder. "I'm sorry about what I said before, about setting up Sonny's killer as a target."

Kelly raised his eyes to hers and she glimpsed the hatred flaring behind his dark irises. "Don't apologize for that," he said. "I'd kill the sorry bastard in a minute if I knew for certain he was the one who murdered Sonny." The look faded away as quickly as it had appeared and he patted her hand reassuringly. "But I promise you, I won't lay a finger on anyone unless I know beyond a shadow of a doubt that they are the guilty party, and, unfortunately, that's not very likely to happen."

Without knowing exactly why she did it, Sherry Mahan leaned over the rocker and gently kissed his cheek. "I believe you," she whispered.

It was growing late.

Johnny shifted uncomfortably on the worn springs of the ancient seat, wondering what could possibly be keeping Marilyn. He glanced through the open window at the red BMW sitting precisely where she had left it and wondered whether she might have left the mall with some friend who had parked on another level. He was an avid student of the girls who spent their time in the malls and knew from observing their habits that they often used the vast garages as convenient meeting places, leaving their own cars safely parked while they went other places with boys.

He frowned at the unpleasant thought, picturing

Marilyn in the backseat of a strange car, doing the evil thing with another boy, someone other than himself. His already florid face turned a deeper shade of red and he vowed to punish her if he discovered that she had been cheating on him.

Marilyn was *his* girl now. She had become his at the moment he spotted her.

Johnny wriggled his huge buttocks around on the seat, wishing she would hurry back. Although his patience was limitless, other considerations were conspiring to make him edgy. For one thing, he had not eaten anything but the Twinkies since early morning, having planned to stop in one of the brightly lit diners along the interstate as soon as he had completed his cursory inspection of the parking garage. That had been hours ago and now his stomach rumbled ominously as he thought of bowls of mashed potatoes covered with rich gravy and a plateful of golden fried chicken.

He had to go to the bathroom, too, but he had been afraid to leave the truck, certain that Marilyn would return and drive away during the few minutes it would take him to make his way to the antiseptic-smelling restroom on the main level of the mall.

A familiar humming noise echoed through the low-ceilinged garage and he slid down in his seat as one of the mall's electric security carts rounded a corner at the far end of the aisle and glided toward him. The cart slowed as it approached the truck and he lay with his face pressed against the worn vinyl for long moments as the security guard flashed the powerful beam of his spotlight into the cab.

Johnny silently rehearsed his story—Waiting for his wife, fell asleep, then he'd laugh and light a cigarette, Damn woman, off spending all his money. . . . If the guard got off the cart and looked down into the cab of the truck, he would have to start explaining, maybe be told to move along.

He would lose Marilyn for sure then, not daring to risk taking her if he had to talk to the guard. The guard would remember him, and tell the cops. The familiar scenario of grim-faced cops interrogating him, black men cornering him in the slammer, played in his head like a frightening movie.

Sweat glistened on his face, darkened the armpits of his faded plaid shirt. The spotlight flashed against the windshield, picking out details of the stained and torn headliner, lingered as if the guard had seen something that aroused his suspicions.

Johnny allowed himself to breathe as the light moved on, flashing against the concrete wall several spaces down from the truck. He heard the reassuring buzz of the electric motor winding up, and cautiously raised himself from the seat, peering over the windowsill just in time to see the security cart turn onto a ramp leading up to the next parking level.

He sat up straight, debating now whether he dared to get out of the truck and relieve himself against the wall. The need to ease the pain of his swollen bladder was becoming unbearable. He placed his hand on the worn door handle, preparing to step out.

Something flashed in the door mirror.

Johnny turned to look back at the entrance leading to the escalators, and promptly forgot about his pain.

Marilyn, her arms loaded down with bright packages, was coming into the garage, her high heels clicking loudly against the concrete.

Johnny quickly swiveled around in his seat, scanning the length of the underground tunnel for approaching cars or other shoppers.

There was nothing.

Grinning happily, and unable to believe his good luck, he quickly stepped out of the truck and raised the hinged lid of the wooden box in the bed, propping it open with a length of broomstick he had cut off specifically for the purpose. Reaching into the box for his bait, he pulled it out of the dirty sack with one fat hand, feeling in the pocket on the bib of his overalls for the small spray bottle he carried there.

Tracy felt better. She and Daisy had lunched together, Daisy telling the most outrageous stories about the Greek sailors who worked on her father's yacht and hinting strongly that an invitation to spend the last two weeks of August cruising the Mediterranean would shortly be forthcoming. Tracy smiled to herself, imagining Trish's reaction. It went without saying that the bitch would try to kill the trip, but she wasn't worried. Daddy would give in as he always did. She allowed herself a vicious grin, thinking of the money she'd spent today.

She shifted the heavy packages, which were beginning to hurt her arms, glad that the BMW was only a few steps away. She really hadn't meant to stay in the mall so long, remembering now that she'd promised to go to a late afternoon swimming party at the country club with Todd Matthews, the golden hunk she'd been dating since school let out for the summer. Not that she was very worried about being late. When Todd saw her in the tiny yellow thong bikini she'd just bought at Saks his eyeballs were going to fall right out on the floor.

She stopped at the rear of the car, fumbling in her purse for her keys. Finding them beneath the cellular phone, she popped the trunk lid open and dumped everything inside. She slammed the trunk lid shut and started around to the driver's door.

That was when she heard the sound.

Tracy stopped in her tracks and listened. A slow smile erased her perpetual pout as the kitten meowed again, a compelling, plaintive wail, as though the poor little thing might be lost or hurt.

Like most girls her age, Tracy Swanson loved kittens.

"Here, kitty!" She looked around for the kitten. "Meow!"

There it was, precariously perched on the edge of an old wooden box on the back of the dirty old truck parked right on the other side of her car.

The tiny gray kitten, which couldn't possibly be more than a few weeks old, meowed again and she saw that one of its little paws was wrapped in a crude bloodstained bandage.

"Poor baby, what happened to you?" she cooed, hurrying around the car and reaching out to the kitten. She wondered how it had managed to get up onto the truck bed all by itself, vaguely recalling the vehicle and its fat driver from earlier in the day.

"Meow!"

Tracy laid her hand on the tiny creature's head, its soft fur like velvet beneath her fingers. The kitten arched against her and she clasped it to her breast, heedless of the stained bandage soiling her pink silk blouse. "Do you want to go home, darling?" she whispered.

"Y-yes!" The strangely resonant voice sounded almost in her ear and she whirled to see the fat man grinning at her, the obscene swell of his filthy overalls brushing against her skirt.

Tracy's eyes widened and she opened her mouth to speak as the fat man raised a small plastic bottle and sprayed something into her face. She inhaled sharply as the pungent cloud of ether filled her lungs. Her knees buckled and the frightened kitten leapt clear of her arms, landing in the backseat of the BMW.

Moving with surprising grace, the fat man easily swept the collapsing girl into his arms. Glancing quickly around the garage to be certain he was not being observed, Johnny lifted her into the wooden box behind the pickup's cab.

Fighting to hold onto the edge of consciousness, Tracy stared up at him from the blankets. He grinned jovially and waggled a fat finger at her.

"B-bad girl!"

She opened her mouth to scream and he sprayed another shot of the nauseating gas directly onto her tongue. She gagged and fell back on the stained blankets at the bottom of the box as he deftly pulled a precut strip of silvery tape from the inside of the opened lid and slapped it across her mouth. He flipped her onto her stomach with a practiced motion and secured her wrists and ankles together with two more pieces of tape.

Turning the unconscious girl back onto her side, and checking to be certain she was still breathing, Johnny stroked her thigh and smiled beatifically. "Marilyn," he crooned.

He reached into the BMW for the kitten, dropped it into the box with Tracy Swanson and lowered the lid, securing it with a shiny padlock.

Moments later, the old pickup rattled out of the Penn Center Mall's parking garage, leaving behind nothing more in the way of evidence than a cloud of greasy smoke and a spreading patch of oil on the concrete floor beside the girl's red car.

CHAPTER 6

Pieces

"SHELLY?"

Chris Kelly leaned closer to the campground's post-mounted pay phone, the only one in the area, trying to hear above the noise of a revving outboard motor on the lake.

"Chris, is that you?" Shelly's voice came over the scratchy line sounding weak and disoriented.

"Yeah, honey, it's me."

"Oh, Chris, it's so terrible. What am I going to do?" The sound of the motor died abruptly and he looked up to see an aluminum fishing boat gliding to the small dock where Sherry was conversing with a heavyset man in overalls and a baseball cap. Shelly's anguished sobs became suddenly louder in his ear. "Chris, are you still there?"

He turned back to the receiver. "Yeah, honey."

"Chris, where are you? Can you come up here?"

"I'm already here, Shelly," he explained. "I was out of the country but I came straight up to the lake as soon as I received your message last night."

Shelly sniffled loudly, emitting a tiny wail. "The lake! Oh, God, Chris. I'd never have left if I'd known. . . ."

"No, no. It's fine. Sherry told me you were totally knocked out. You needed to get away."

"You met Sherry?" Shelly's voice seemed calmer.

He cut his eyes to the edge of the lake. Sherry was walking into the woods with the man in the overalls. He frowned, wondering where they were going. "She's nice, isn't she, Chris?"

He turned his attention back to the phone. "Yeah, honey, she's very nice."

"Shall I come back up there tonight, Chris?" Shelly's voice was hopeful.

Kelly felt a sudden surge of panic. He wasn't sure he could face his cousin right now, not with the knowledge that Sonny's body was still in the pool. A momentary vision of the nibbling trout filled his mind and he felt a wave of nausea sweeping over him.

"What did the doctor say?" he asked. "You were supposed to go to the doctor, weren't you?"

Shelly sighed. "I went. He said I should rest," she complained. "They keep trying to dope me up. . . . Chris, I can have Mike drive me. He's got his license now, you know."

"Look, Shelly," Chris said sternly. "The doctor's right. You've got to get some rest. Mike and Chris need you now.

"Besides, there's really nothing you can do up here right now. Sherry's here with me and the two of us are going to spend some time going over the whole area with a fine-tooth comb." He hesitated. "We need someone down there by the phone," he lied, "just in case we turn up anything."

"Oh, Chris, do you think there's any chance you'll find him?" She was openly pleading for something, anything, to hang on to.

"Sonny is dead, Shelly. He's been missing too long for anything else to make sense." He hated himself for saying the words and cringed in preparation for her tearful response.

"I know," she said quietly. "I guess I've really known it all along."

"Sherry and I are going to try to figure out what happened to him."

"Will you do something for me, Chris?"

"If I can, honey."

Her voice cracked on the line. "Find Sonny and bring him home to me and the boys . . . so we can bury him by his dad and mother." She sobbed again and he could hear her composure going. "Oh, Chris, I couldn't bear it if he just disappeared from our lives like . . . like Diana."

"I promise, Shelly. We'll bring Sonny home." He looked around the campground for Sherry. She was nowhere to be seen. "Can you put Mike on for a minute?" he asked.

"Uncle Chris?" His nephew's voice came on

the line strong and clear and Kelly realized he no longer sounded like the gangly teenager he always envisioned when he thought of the boy.

"Hi, Mike, you and your brother okay?"

"We're okay," said the boy, "but Mom's not doing so good. She just cries all the time. Are you guys coming down here pretty soon?"

"Pretty soon," he said. "We want to look around a little more. Look, do you feel up to answering a few questions for me? I already know that you and Chris were the last ones to see your dad."

"Yeah, but we already told the search guys everything that happened that day. I mean, there wasn't really anything to tell."

Kelly nodded. "Okay, Mike. How about before that? Did anything strange ever happen when you were up here working around the hotel? Anybody hanging around, anything ever missing, stuff like that?"

There was a long silence on the line. "Geez, I don't think so," Mike finally answered. "I mean, people used to break into the hotel all the time before we started going up there. You know, to do dope and stuff, but nothing ever happened after we changed the locks and started cleaning the place up, except for that thing with the furniture."

The sun was dropping low over the mountain now, plunging the woods surrounding the lake into deep shadow. There was still no sign of Sherry and the fat man.

"What about the furniture, Mike?"

"Well, the second or third weekend we went up to the lake at the beginning of the summer, Dad said there was some furniture missing, an old wardrobe and a couple of tables and chairs. He'd counted everything the time before that and insisted there was supposed to be more."

"What happened?"

"Nothing," said Mike. "Mom told him if he hadn't been drinking so much Iron City beer he would've got the count right the first time." He laughed. "Boy, did he get mad. I mean, you would've thought the old stuff was worth money or something."

Kelly laughed. "Okay, there was some missing furniture. Anything else?"

"Well, there was some other stuff missing, too—old boxes and glass jugs and junk like that, from the kitchen. Dad said he didn't care about that, though, because he was going to throw it all out anyway."

"That all?"

"Yeah, I think so. Oh, yeah, there was this old truck. That was pretty weird."

Kelly felt his heart skip. "What old truck, Mike?"

"Well, the same weekend that we found the other stuff missing there was this really old pickup parked in the shed down by the lake. At first we figured some fishermen had left it there for the day, but it was still there when we left on Sunday. The next time we came back it was gone."

"Do you remember what it looked like?"

"It was real old, kind of dark colored. I really didn't pay very much attention to it." He paused, thinking. "There was writing on the side, but it was all muddy and you couldn't really read it. Dad thought it was an old taxi."

Chris frowned. "I never heard of anyone using a truck as a taxi."

"That's what I told him," Mike replied.

Tracy Swanson was on the verge of hysteria.

She had awakened some minutes earlier to the sound of wind whistling across the flat top of the wooden box in which she was imprisoned, bound and gagged. Smelly blankets pressed against the side of her face and there was a terrible metallic taste in her mouth. She thought she might throw up and was terrified that if she did she would choke on her own vomit.

The floor she was lying on was hard beneath the blankets and something sharp poked uncomfortably into her side every time the speeding vehicle bounced.

Tracy struggled ineffectually against her bonds again and fell back, exhausted, trying to remember exactly what had happened. She clearly remembered coming out of the mall after shopping with Daisy Vandeveer. After that, however, everything went fuzzy.

The truck bounced again and the thing poking her side jabbed her cruelly in the ribs. She closed her eyes and began to weep. Something hot and wet touched her face and she screamed through her gag.

She opened her eyes to find the little gray kitten licking her cheek.

The kitten!

It all came rushing back to her: The kitten and the old truck and . . . the man, the horrible, smelly old man. She remembered him lifting her, his rotten breath worse than whatever he had sprayed into her face to knock her out . . . and his touch—fat, disgustingly filthy fingers caressing her thigh.

Tracy screamed again, ripping desperately at the bonds that held her hands behind her back.

Useless.

There was a little gray light coming in through a series of small holes in the side of the box and she could see that there was room to sit up. She struggled, twisting herself awkwardly around until her back was pressed against the rough wooden side of the box. Her silk blouse snagged on a splinter and she heard it rip as she worked her way to a sitting position. Her struggles had hiked her short skirt up over her hips and she tried moving around to work it lower. It climbed higher still.

The kitten crawled into her lap and curled up in a contented ball.

Tracy tried to pull her thoughts together. She was not an unintelligent girl and it had already occurred to her that she was being kidnapped by the fat man. He must have been watching her, waiting in the garage for the right moment to take her.

There was no doubt in her mind that her father would pay whatever ransom was asked. She tried to comfort herself with the thought that it was just a matter of time until he was contacted and paid for her release. All she had to do was keep her head. When it was over, she supposed, her picture would be in all of the papers and her father would give her anything she wanted to make up for her ordeal.

The truck lurched again and began slowing and a horrible thought crept into her mind. Suppose the fat man hadn't taken her for money at all? Suppose he had taken her because he'd been so pissed off over the way she'd screamed at him in the garage? Suppose he was taking her to some lonely place intent only on raping and murdering her?

She began to cry again.

The truck bounced sharply, driving the irritating object into her ribs. She strained to see in the dim light, trying to figure out what kept jabbing her, saw her red Gucci bag, still tucked under her arm, the thin leather strap twisted across her shoulder.

Tracy's eyes widened as she realized that her cellular phone was right there in the bag. If she could only free her hands and reach it . . .

The truck made a sharp turn, throwing her painfully back onto her side. The kitten meowed in fright and scampered to the corner of the box as the old springs began to creak and bounce, as if they had just turned onto a rutted, unpaved road.

Ignoring the pain in her side, Tracy struggled with new energy to slip her hands free from the tight bonds encircling her wrists.

A fine curtain of dust filtered into the box through the air holes.

Sherry Mahan stood on a narrow dirt road behind the campground's log-fronted general store, talking to the fat man in the overalls.

"Now, if you and your mister are thinkin' about takin' one of my cabins in August," he said, pointing to a row of rooftops higher up on the slope among the trees, "you'll have to put in a reservation pretty soon. Everything fills up real fast from round about the first of August until Labor Day. That's when we hold the fishin' tournament."

His name was Jake Coolidge and he claimed to have been running the campground since '46 when he'd returned to Lake Lazarus after serving as a young private in the Pacific. By his own account, he'd never strayed more than fifty miles from the place since that time. In addition to running the campground, the cabins, and the general store, Jake was also the postmaster and constable.

In the twenty minutes since she had begun talking to him, presenting herself and Chris as a pair of vacationing teachers with an interest in local history, Sherry had heard the encapsulated histories of half the families in the area, learning, among other things, that there were a lot more people living in the mountains around the isolated lake than she would have imagined.

Many of the residents of Lake Lazarus were, like Jake himself, direct descendants of the original settlers who had come to the area in the early 1800s to hunt and trap. Unfortunately, half the men he had so far described sounded like ideal candidates for her list of suspects in Sonny's disappearance; loners who roamed the woods hunting out of season, growing a little dope in inaccessible plots on the steep mountainsides, logging or hiring on to Forest Service crews as the mood and the need for cash moved them.

"It's such a beautiful little lake," she remarked, looking pointedly at the sun sinking over the water, and hoping to change the subject to the area surrounding the old hotel on the far shore. "What about that beautiful old white building we saw down at the other end?"

She was interrupted by the squeaking of springs and a revving engine. Jake pulled her to the side of the narrow road and they watched an elderly pickup truck drive by. "'Lo, Johnny," called Jake. "How's them Twinkies of yours holdin' out?"

The fat man at the wheel grinned and held up a cellophane package.

Jake shook his head as the truck disappeared into the woods. "Now, there's a sad case for you," he said. "That poor boy's daddy was probably the most prosperous feller in these parts at one time."

Sherry looked mildly interested.

"Yessir, finest taxidermist in the Northeast," Jake continued. "Folks used to send skins and trophies from as far away as Africa and Alaska for old John Skinner to mount." He reached into his overall pocket and scooped out a chaw of shredded tobacco, which he stuffed into his mouth. "Poor feller got kilt in a huntin' accident years back," he mumbled. "Blowed his head clean off—" He stared at Sherry and suddenly flushed a deep red. "Beg pardon, ma'am. Didn't mean to go talkin' like that to no pretty young schoolteacher like yourself."

Sherry smiled. "That's perfectly all right," she replied. "I don't suppose there's much call for taxidermy these days anyway."

"Oh, you'd be surprised," Jake said around a mouthful of tobacco. "Come deer season there's always some call. Leastways, enough to keep young Johnny going for the rest of the year. Not a half-bad taxidermist when he gets the chance. Sad part is the boy's kinda slow, if ya know what I mean." He touched his forehead meaningfully with an index finger. "Folks round these parts used to tease him somethin' fierce when he was just a little feller. He's all alone up there in that cabin now that his mama's gone." He spit a wad of juice into the dust and shook his head again. "Just him and all them stuffed animals of his."

Sherry nodded. "You were telling me about the building at the end of the lake," she persisted.

Jake laughed. "The old Summerland Hotel? Now, there's some stories I could tell you about that old barn. Most folks think she was built by the mob during Prohibition, but that ain't it at all."

"No?" Sherry raised her eyebrows.

"Oh, the mob owned it for a while, all right." Jake chuckled. "Used to land their seaplanes right here on the lake, bringin' in hooch from Canada, don't ya see? Dug 'em a whole network of rooms underneath and run a casino and speakeasy down there," he said. "Even had escape tunnels run up into the mountain for the customers, in case of raids by the police."

"Really, I had no idea."

"Oh, the Summerland was somethin' back in them days," he said. "'Course she was built way before that by a couple of rich New Yorkers who just wanted a nice place to come fishin'. Back in the 1890s, I believe."

"That's fascinating," said Sherry. She spied Kelly coming through the trees beside the store and waved. "Hi, honey, over here!"

Kelly joined them and she linked her arm through his. "Mr. Coolidge was just telling me some fascinating things about the old hotel at the end of the lake," she said.

Kelly nodded agreeably and looked interested.

"Some bad business down there just recently about that Lasco feller," said Jake. "Him and his missus was gonna reopen the place. Then he up and disappeared." He shook his big head. "We was all hopin' he'd get the Summerland goin' again and bring some money back to Lake Lazarus." He looked around and lowered his voice to a confidential tone. "'Course, some say that end of the lake always has been jinxed," he added.

"Oh, in what way?" Kelly asked.

Jake shrugged. "Disappearances. First them two convicts, now Lasco." He loosed another spurt of tobacco juice against the trunk of a tree. "Then there was those hunters back in '85 and them two young college girls in '79."

Kelly and Sherry exchanged glances.

"Say, can we buy you a beer?" asked Kelly.

Jake grinned. "Don't mind if I do," he said. He led them around to a picnic table in front of the store and extracted a six-pack from an ice chest. "Oh, I could tell you some stories about that end of the lake down there."

Kelly laid a twenty on the scarred wood surface and Coolidge popped the tops on three cans of Iron City. "Well, we'd sure like to hear all about it," he said.

CHAPTER 7

Puzzles

THE slatted wooden door creaked open, illuminating the jumbled main room of the small cabin in the final rays of the setting sun. The feeble red light shone on the dusty heads of dozens of animals, large and small, fierce and passive, all staring down onto a filthy floor strewn with a month-long accumulation of crumpled food wrappers and empty soda cans. The raucous sound effects of a cartoon show blared from a scarred console TV nearly buried beneath an avalanche of comic books in one corner.

The TV screen was streaked with dust, its control knobs smeared with particles of food. The television had not been turned off for more than a year.

Johnny stepped into the foul-smelling room, tiptoeing daintily around piles of refuse in his muddy clogs. He crossed the center of the room, detached a can of orange soda from a six-pack on the battered table, and popped the metal tab on its top.

Orange soda dribbled out from the corners of his mouth, splashing onto the front of his overalls as he drained the can in a single gargantuan swallow. He tossed the empty onto the floor and opened another, consuming half of it in another giant swallow. His thirst finally slaked, he uttered an ear-splitting belch and sank onto the greasy, sprung sofa to think.

There were so many things to do now that he had Marilyn. This was the first time he had taken a girl without being fully prepared beforehand and things were beginning to get confusing. He didn't have her eyes yet and he couldn't remember if he needed more chemicals for the delicate flaying and tanning processes ahead. Also, it had occurred to him when he was more than halfway back to the lake that he no longer had a suitable place to keep the girl while she was still living. He had previously always used one of the many rooms in the old hotel before carrying his girls down to the kitchen for preparation.

Johnny clasped the sides of his head with his hands, trying to make his brain work faster. He wished he could read and write so he could make lists of all the things he was supposed to do and remember. He couldn't read and write, however, so everything had to be kept in his head. He squeezed his eyes shut, trying to visualize the contents of the shelves in his supply cabinet.

It was very hard.

He knew, for instance, that he had come into the cabin just now for a very specific reason. There was something he needed to get and he had intended to be there for just a minute. All the other thoughts bumping around inside his head had made him forget what he had come for.

A loud, whistling noise shrilled into the room, causing Johnny to look up. An old *Road Runner* cartoon was playing on the television.

Johnny grinned.

The Road Runner was one of his favorites.

He focused his delighted attention on the screen as Wile E. Coyote prepared an elaborate trap beside a dusty desert highway. A giant firecracker was set to go off just as the speedy Road Runner stopped to peck at a plate of food in the middle of the highway. Johnny slurped his orange soda and clamped his hand over his mouth in anticipation, waiting to see how the trap was going to backfire on the stupid coyote.

Maybe if he relaxed for a few minutes he could remember what he had come to the cabin for.

A draft of cold, pine-scented air swept across Tracy Swanson's face and her eyelids fluttered open. Above her, the outline of the wooden box framed a patch of darkening blue sky that was just beginning to be studded with sparkling points of starlight. The lid of the box had been propped open with some sort of a stick.

She had finally cried herself to sleep some-time earlier, following a painful and futile strug-gle to free her hands in the bouncing truck. Now she cringed miserably in a corner of the box, waiting for the fat man to appear and do what-ever he had planned for her.

She lay waiting in the dark for several more minutes, the sky above her gradually going from deep blue to velvety black, the stars growing brighter and more numerous. When nothing happened she painfully worked herself into a kneeling position and peered out over the top of the box.

The truck was angled in against a steep embankment at the end of a dirt road. Tall pine trees, their overhanging branches nearly devoid of color in the growing darkness, surrounded the road on both sides.

A screech of laughter sounded through the forest and Tracy looked up the embankment. The dark outline of a small house was etched against the massive bulk of a heavily wooded mountainside. The front door of the house stood open and blue light flickered out onto the ground-level porch. Another strange howl sounded from within the house, followed by a string of jangled musical notes.

Tracy's eyes scanned the area around the truck, finally coming to rest upon a huge wood-pile. To one side of the pile, a large section of a tree stump sat on the ground. Starlight glittered on the blade of a double-edged ax stuck firmly into its top.

Glancing fearfully at the house, Tracy turned her back to the side of the box and levered herself up until she was sitting on the edge with her feet still inside. The kitten meowed loudly from the far corner and she prayed the sound would not carry to the house.

Bound hand and foot as she was, she teetered precariously on the edge, feeling the rough wood biting into the soft skin of her buttocks. There was nothing to aid her balance except the lid of the box on its flimsy prop, and she felt sure it would come crashing down on her if she touched it. She twisted her head around, trying to gauge the distance to the ground, hoping to swing her legs up out of the box, and then to jump down from there. If she could only hop the twenty feet to where the ax was buried in the stump, she was sure she could free herself.

She froze as the sounds from the house suddenly went silent, briefly considering slipping back into the temporary security of the box. She expected to see the fat man step through the door of the house at any moment. If he should see her trying to escape . . .

The raucous music resumed and she took a deep breath through her nose, certain that waiting for the man to return was the worst possible thing she could do. She was convinced that he meant to kill her and she wasn't going to wait around to find out how. The sharp edge of the box bit painfully into her flesh as she lifted her legs preparatory to swinging them over.

The kitten suddenly yowled at her feet and she

overbalanced, falling over backward. Her feet hit the broomstick supporting the heavy lid and it slammed shut with a loud bang as she toppled to the ground, screaming behind her gag.

A blinding jolt of pain shot though Tracy's shoulder and she lay whimpering beside the truck, her face and golden hair half buried in the cold mud. She raised her head, expecting to see the fat man looming over her, but saw nothing but dirt. Her view of the house was blocked by the embankment.

As her head cleared she suddenly realized that if she could not see the house, then its occupant could not see her. Heartened by this tiny turn of good luck, she scrambled to her knees and, pressing her back against the side of the truck, got unsteadily to her feet. She looked down, realizing that she was still wearing her red heels. Kicking her feet awkwardly, she managed to get them off and her toes sank into the soft mud. She leaned forward and hopped a few inches experimentally. Her mind filled with an image of how pathetically ridiculous she must look.

For the first time in as long as she could remember, Tracy Swanson did not care.

"T-bone steaks?" Kelly stood by the smoking barbecue grill at the edge of the lake, staring. Sherry posed on the veranda above him holding up the steaks like two prize specimens in a contest.

"Where did you get them?" he asked suspiciously. "The only thing resembling meat that I saw in that camp store had Oscar Meyer written on the package."

She grinned innocently. "That nice old Mr. Coolidge had them tucked away in his cooler. He said he wanted us to have them."

Kelly was incredulous. "*Nice old Mr. Coolidge* wanted us to have them? The old skinflint kept my twenty bucks for four beers, two of which he drank himself!"

She smiled and brought the steaks down to him. He plopped them onto the grill with a satisfying sizzle. "You just have to learn how to talk to people, Chris," she said mysteriously.

"Okay, out with it, how'd you con the old man out of the steaks?"

She smiled sweetly. "Well, I might have mentioned that we were on our honeymoon and hadn't realized we wouldn't be able to find anything special up here for our first dinner."

He clucked his tongue in disapproval. "Are all the cops in Bremerton as crooked as you are?" he asked.

She shrugged. "Hey, I was hungry. I like my steak rare, by the way."

He turned the steaks and reached into a cooler on the grass for a pair of beers. He handed one to her and looked out over the lake. A few lights flickered dimly in the direction of the campground. "So what do you make of old Coolidge's theory that this end of the lake is jinxed?" he asked. "You don't think that could have anything to do with Sonny?"

Sherry had been nearly silent on the drive back from the campground, responding to his queries and speculations with a series of grunts and one-word answers that indicated she was deep in thought. He hadn't pressed her for conversation, deciding to wait until now.

She took a sip of her beer and checked to see that the meat wasn't burning. "I think it has everything to do with Sonny," she said, turning to face him.

"Yeah, but on the other hand, people are always getting lost in wilderness areas," he countered. "You said yourself it happened all the time when you were out in Los Angeles."

"Getting lost, yes. *Not* disappearing without a trace."

"You mean, they always get found, eventually."

"Not always," she replied, "but usually. For six people to disappear in an area like this without any of them ever turning up again simply defies the laws of probability." She gazed out over the water and her voice took on a faraway quality. "That's six people that we *know* of," she emphasized.

"I'm not sure what you're getting at," he said. "You think there might be more?"

She nodded. "Maybe a lot more."

He waited.

"Coolidge got me thinking," she said after a long pause. "Six people have disappeared around here over roughly a fifteen-year period. No traces were ever found of any of them, and no criminal investigations of any consequence were ever conducted. They were all just listed as missing persons: a lost hunter, missing campers, and so forth."

"Yeah?" He was having a hard time seeing where this was leading. He turned to the grill and flipped the steaks.

"Over the past several years the state troopers here and in New York and Jersey have mapped out an area they call Phantomland. Within this area, which stretches east to Philadelphia and Newark, south as far as Harrisburg, and well up into New York State, there have been a sizable series of unsolved disappearances, mostly from in and around large shopping malls.

"Unofficially, the troopers think the disappearances are the work of one serial murderer. They call him the Phantom because, so far at least, neither he nor any of his victims have ever been seen. He takes them without leaving a single trace. Nothing. They just disappear. In fact, the only thing that links all the cases together is the fact that the victims are all young, all female, and all taken from busy shopping centers with lots of people around."

"And you think they're connected with what's been going on up here?" he asked.

"On a map of Phantomland," she said, "Lake Lazarus and Bremerton are at roughly the geographic center."

Kelly felt a sudden chill run down his spine. He stared at the meat on the grill, oblivious to the fact that it was charring around the edges.

"This has been going on for how long?" He phrased the question slowly and deliberately.

Sherry shrugged. "It's really hard to say. You see, the various police agencies involved have only been comparing these kinds of records for a few years." She laughed bitterly. "Believe it or not," she said, "up until very recently, few people in law enforcement even believed there was such a thing as serial murder. That's how creeps like Ted Bundy managed to go for so long without getting caught, by simply moving from jurisdiction to jurisdiction without anyone ever noticing the patterns." She stared at the grill, which was beginning to flame. "Hey, you're incinerating our dinner!"

Kelly snatched the meat off the flames. It made perfect sense. A serial killer operating from an isolated area like this, bringing his victims into the mountains for disposal, silencing and disposing of any locals who happened to stumble across his secret.

A Phantom.

He was probably hiding the bodies in the numerous caves that dotted the mountains at this end of the lake.

An incident from his early days in Vietnam flashed into Kelly's memory. A mission he had been sent to observe during his in-country familiarization.

He looked at Sherry, who was scooping salad onto plates beside the blackened steaks. "Would it be too much trouble for you to run me back over to the campground after dinner?"

She held his plate out to him. "Think you're going to need those hot dogs after all?

He shook his head. "No. But I do think you may be onto something. I'd like to make a phone call or two."

She raised her eyebrows, waiting for him to say more.

"If your theory is correct," he continued, "there's some specialized equipment I might be able to borrow that'll help us get to the bottom of it." He paused, wondering how much of his embryonic plan to let her in on. He didn't want the local police blundering in before he had a chance to track down the killer—if one really existed in these woods—and confirm the horrible nagging suspicion that had been taking root in his mind ever since Sherry had raised the specter of a faceless serial killer whose activities centered in the Bremerton area. "It might not hurt if we were a little better armed, as well," he casually added.

CHAPTER 8

Bad Girl

T H E cartoon ended in a crescendo of explosions as Wile E. Coyote stupidly ran through the shooting gallery he had set up by the side of the road and was blasted to smithereens.

Johnny stretched contentedly and tossed his third empty orange soda can onto the floor with a clank. A noisy commercial promoting Barbie dolls living in a cute little plastic house began and he stared at it in fascination. The little girls in the commercial were moving their Barbies around from the living room to the bedroom, giving them showers, dressing them, and fixing their hair. In a way, Johnny realized, his girls were like Barbies. His own personal collection of grown-up Barbies. He smiled, wondering what the Mattel people would think if they could see his collection.

The commercial ended and was replaced by

another in which he had no interest. He scratched his chest and thought about someday naming one of his girls Barbie. . . .

Marilyn. He remembered that she was still out in the truck. She had been asleep when he had checked on her before and he had been afraid for a minute that he had given her too much ether in the shopping center. He hadn't intended to spray the chemical into her mouth, but she had opened it to scream at just the wrong moment.

He had felt up under her pretty silk blouse to be sure she was still breathing, thrilling to the beating of her heart beneath the hot, smooth skin of her breast. Leaving the lid of the box propped open to be sure she got some fresh air, he had come into the cabin to get something.

He turned around, scanning the cluttered room for the thing he wanted and spied it behind the dusty glass of a tall cabinet in the corner—the cabinet that had been his father's. Smiling because he had finally remembered what he wanted after watching the cartoon, he crossed the room to the cabinet, opening it reverently and gazing at the precious objects inside. He tried to decide which of them to take, worrying at the same time that Marilyn would be getting chilled in the open air. He didn't like taking his father's prized possessions out of the cabinet, but knew he might need one before Marilyn's preparation was complete.

Better safe than sorry. That was what his mother always used to say.

Better safe than sorry.

* * *

Tracy crouched shivering by the stump. Her shoulders were cruelly twisted, the pain shooting in sharp jolts to her neck as she held her wrists centered on the exposed portion of the rusty ax blade, sawing slowly though the tough fabric of the heavy duct tape.

She wanted to scream.

It had taken her nearly five minutes to make her way to the stump after she had fallen down again, landing face first in the mud five feet from the truck and crawling the rest of the way on her belly. Now, her clothes and body coated in the cold, slimy stuff, her teeth chattering so hard she was sure they would break, she felt her bonds beginning to part at last.

Tracy closed her eyes and sawed harder, driving herself beyond limits of endurance she had not known she possessed with visions of the terrible fat man who, she was convinced, would be back to get her momentarily. The sound of the cartoon music from the cabin had stopped moments before, replaced by a jolly commercial jingle, and she rolled her eyes toward the dirt embankment, praying that the big moron would stay where he was for just a few seconds longer.

The tape parted with a ripping sound and she held her chafed wrists out in front of her, hardly able to believe that she was free. Dropping gracelessly onto her rear end, she tore at the bonds securing her ankles, breaking off several expensively manicured nails in the process. Her feet came apart at last and she stood unsteadily, looking around the small clearing like a frightened animal. Except for the narrow dirt road leading off into the dark tunnel of the trees, the surrounding forest seemed to press in on all sides. There was no light anywhere to indicate any sign of civilization.

"Get out!" she screamed to herself silently. "Run!" She had a fleeting thought about taking the ax with her for protection, made a half-hearted attempt to wrench it from the stump. It would not budge. Hobbling to the truck, she retrieved her shoes from the mud: straightened to see starlight gleaming on the open padlock hanging from the shiny hasp secured to the box. Acting on a sudden burst of inspiration, she snapped the lock shut. The little gray kitten meowed piteously from inside the box and she felt a sudden pang of regret that she had not saved it, too.

Climbing up onto the running board of the truck, Tracy looked up at the cabin beyond the embankment, saw a huge shadow moving through the blue light at the door. She emitted a strangled little cry of terror and ran down the dirt road in her stockinged feet. Her red high heels clutched in one hand, the Gucci bag flapping from her shoulder, she disappeared into the darkness.

Chris Kelly stood by the pay phone in the campground, illuminated in the glare of a huge bonfire down by the lake. Nearby, Sherry stood in the shadows beneath a cluster of pines watching the antics of a group of middle-aged men dressed up in Indian war paint who were performing a ridiculous initiation ritual that involved lots of chanting and banging of drums.

The phone clicked and Blackstone's voice came back on the line. "Chris, are you still there?"

Kelly clapped his free hand over his ear in order to hear over the chanting. "I'm here, Mr. Black."

"I think I've got all the items you wanted. How would you like them delivered?"

Kelly hesitated. He was tempted to ask for the helicopter that had brought him to the lake but didn't want to risk the killer spotting it, as Sherry had the previous night. "Well, I don't want to attract any attention up here," he said. "What can you suggest?"

Blackstone laughed. "How about Federal Express?"

"Federal Express?" He was sure the old man was joking.

"Certainly," said Blackstone, his voice serious. "They're absolutely reliable and we have a special account with them. Is there a commercial airport near you?"

"Bremerton, Pennsylvania," he replied. "It's between the lake and the city, not more than twenty miles from here."

"I'm going to turn you over to one of our shipping coordinators in a minute," said Blackstone. "He'll have your goods to you in the morning."

"I appreciate this very much," said Kelly.

Blackstone's voice took on a concerned note. Kelly had briefly outlined the situation for him earlier and the old man was obviously having reservations about letting him pursue it on his own. "Are you sure you wouldn't like some backup, Chris? Tracking dangerous game through the woods isn't exactly your field of expertise."

"We're not planning on taking this cat," said Chris, following Blackstone's veiled way of speaking over open phone lines. "We just want to determine if he's actually holing up in the area without spooking him."

Blackstone sounded dubious. "Is that why you need the G.I. Joe kit?"

"Precautions," said Kelly with more conviction than he actually felt. The G.I. Joe kit was the agency's designation for an individual light-assault pack, which included, among other toys, an automatic assault rifle, flak jacket, and stun grenades. "We're treading on dangerous ground here and if we do stumble across our friend, I'd like something a little more substantial than what we currently have on hand."

"All right." Blackstone sighed. "You've been around long enough to know what you're doing. Just don't get yourself into anything you can't handle. I need you back here in one piece as soon as you can manage it."

"A new assignment?"

"A very touchy proposition," said Blackstone. "A project that only you can handle properly."

Kelly looked out over the blazing campfire. A year ago he would have been flattered by Blackstone's admission that he was top reaper. Now . . . The men, a bunch of average guys away from the wives and kids for a weekend, and obviously having a good time, were dancing around it in a circle, pausing to crack open cans of beer and daub each other's faces with war paint.

The mingled smells of grilling hamburgers and the clean, sweet scent of pine pervaded the cold night air. Sherry's face glowed in the firelight, highlights shining in her hair.

"I'll take care of this matter and be back down to get started in a few days," he lied, afraid that Blackstone might pull his support if he told him the truth.

He had already decided that he was not going to kill anyone ever again.

With the possible exception of the Phantom.

Johnny walked down the embankment toward the truck, stopping to squint down at it in the darkness. Something was not right. He unslung his father's lovingly polished and oiled .30-caliber carbine from his shoulder and pumped a cautionary round into the chamber. He seldom removed the precious rifle from its sealed cabinet with the rest of his father's guns. He had last used it when the two drunken hunters had intruded into one of his hideaways and seen the freshly skinned body of Veronica hanging from the hook before he'd had an opportunity to take her down to the cold room.

Fortunately, he had had the carbine with him then, the hunters' presence at the south end of the lake prompting him to be extra cautious, as he was being now, knowing the strange man and woman were still at the hotel. Even at that it had been a close thing with the hunters. He'd spent a whole night stalking them through the woods—his woods—surprising them at dawn, just as they had thought they were safe.

Johnny stroked the gleaming stock of the carbine, remembering how the hunters had looked, each with a single bullet in his brain. Killing them had been . . . satisfying, almost as satisfying as shopping in the malls.

Johnny grinned. For some strange reason that was beyond his comprehension, no one ever expected a fat, clumsy oaf like him to be an expert shot.

He reached the truck in a crouch, the carbine held at high port, ready to swing instantly onto any target that might present itself. He scanned the clearing near the woodpile, his sharp little eyes darting suspiciously over the stump and the stacks of deadfall waiting to be cut, the dark tree line beyond.

Forest sounds.

The slight rustle of wind in the treetops.

Satisfied that no one was lurking in the shadows, he turned back to examine the truck itself. Hadn't he left the lid of the box open so that

Marilyn could get plenty of fresh air? He thought he had.

Johnny slowly lowered the rifle and fingered the securely fastened padlock on the box. The kitten meowed inside the box. Berating himself for his own forgetfulness, he clicked the carbine on safe, stowed it in the cab and climbed into the driver's seat. He started the engine, turned on the lights and backed the truck around in a half circle. He was just about to shift into first gear when he noticed something directly ahead illuminated in the glare of the headlights. He stared at the thing on the ground for a long moment, trying to decide whether it was worth getting out and examining.

Tracy Swanson was running, her feet, already bloody and numb, slapping along the cold muddy road as she drove herself relentlessly forward. She had stopped once, halting in the deep shadows of a thicket to fumble the cellular phone out of her purse and dial 911. The tiny portable had blinked maddeningly in her hand, the glowing keyboard flashing a message that indicated no cellular signal was being received. She looked up at the black mountains towering around her, remembering vaguely that high hills blocked the portable phones.

Cursing and weeping at the unfairness of her predicament, she had forced herself back out onto the road, running and sobbing. After several tortured minutes the road crested a small rise and the trees thinned ahead of her, allowing a view of a shining body of water in the moonlight. She paused, gasping for breath and hardly able to believe her eyes. The glow of a roaring bonfire lit the shoreline half a mile away and she could hear the distant sound of voices.

It sounded like chanting.

Tracy had been praying—honestly, fervently praying. Now she thanked God for having answered her prayers. There were people down there. People who would help her, make her warm, and call her father to come and take her home.

She promised God that if he really got her out of this she wouldn't be such a little bitch anymore.

Not even to Trish.

"Well?" Sherry looked up from her spot by the trees as Kelly walked up with his hands jammed in his pockets.

"Everything we need will be here in the morning. I'll have to go down to the airport to pick it up." He pointed his chin at the bonfire. The dancing had broken up and the revelers were busily engaged in spraying beer on each other. "Exactly what are they doing?"

She laughed. "Just plain raising hell as far as I can tell. If they were back down in town I'd have to arrest the lot of them for disturbing the peace."

He smirked. "Looks like fun."

"Looks like meaningless macho bullshit to me."

"Yeah, well, remember that next time you go to a bridal shower," he retorted.

She punched him on the shoulder.

"Hey, that hurt!"

"You had it coming," she said. "Bridal showers are important stuff!"

"So what do you want to do now?" he asked.

She slipped her hand into his. "Well," she said seductively, "I thought we might go back to the hotel. . . ."

He raised his eyebrows. "Yeah, and?"

"And see if we could find the way into those secret tunnels that Coolidge told me about," she said.

"Secret tunnels."

"Yeah, the ones the bootleggers built during prohibition."

"Great." He shrugged.

"What did you think I meant?" She was grinning.

"Nothing."

"Come on."

"Nothing."

"I know what was on your dirty little mind."

He dropped her hand and put his hands on his hips. "What?"

"Never mind." Sherry bit her lip to suppress the self-satisfied smirk that was threatening to break out. She had already decided that they were going to sleep together. Now she was sure it was what he wanted, too. She thought

about Sonny and realized that this was the
worst possible time to be thinking about love-
making. To hell with it. Maybe that was the
reason she felt the need to be held and loved,
to drive away the nightmare if just for a little
while. "Come on," she said, laughing and
breaking into a run, "I'll race you back to the
car."

Tracy leaned against a slender sapling at the
crest of the road. Below her she could see the
roofs of a group of rustic buildings clustered at
the water's edge. The bonfire she had glimpsed
through the trees earlier was blazing brightly
and she could clearly make out the features of
the men standing around drinking beer and
talking.

Straightening her skirt and wiping a muddy
forearm across her face, she stepped into the
center of the road and started down the hill
toward the camp. A neon sign in the window of
a little store glowed warmly, conjuring up
visions of hot coffee and food. She tottered forward on her swollen feet, imagining the fuss
they would make when she stumbled in with her
tale of horror. That set her thinking about the
hysteria that would accompany her return
home. She could almost see the headlines,
"Debutante Outwits Kidnapper."

She allowed herself a little smile. Everyone
was going to be so jealous. . . .

Creak, kercreak, creak . . .

Tracy's steps faltered and she turned to look over her shoulder. The old pickup truck, its lights turned off, was gliding along behind her, the rusty springs squeaking as it negotiated a rut in the road.

It stopped suddenly and the fat man stepped out of the truck, holding the rifle in one dirty hand. In the other he held up the tattered remains of the silvery tape with which he had bound her hands and feet. He leered at her with his crooked yellow teeth.

"B-bad girl!"

Tracy screamed once before he was on her.

"What was that?"

"What?" Kelly looked up from the hood of Sherry's Mustang. They had run all the way back to the car from the lakefront, sprawling against the car to catch their breath.

Sherry straightened up and looked toward the woods, listening. "I thought I heard a scream."

As if to confirm her observation several high-pitched whoops rang out through the trees and a trio of drunken revelers from the bonfire ran past the car waving cans of beer.

"You did." Chris laughed, watching as the drunks stumbled up a path to a row of cabins.

Sherry shook her head. "This sounded different, like a woman's scream."

They both listened for a moment longer. A couple of teenaged girls in shorts and sweatshirts appeared out of the trees and hurried past them on their way to the store. "Guess I'm getting a little jumpy," she said, opening the car door."

"Save it for tomorrow," he smiled. "Nothing's going to happen tonight."

Search

" **I** give up." Sherry sighed and backed out of the narrow opening hidden behind the paneling under the main stairway leading down into the lobby. Her blond hair was dusted with cobwebs and there was a black smudge across her cheek. "If there's a secret passage under this hotel, whoever built it was smarter than I am."

Kelly flashed the beam of the powerful light he'd bought at the camp store into the dark space. The old timbers were stained black with a patina of age. "Sounds to me like those stories were made up by old Coolidge for the benefit of the tourists." He grinned, pulling the paneling back into place and turning to face her.

They had been going over the lower floor of the hotel for more than three hours without locating anything remotely resembling an entrance to the secret rooms the old man had claimed existed. There had been a moment's excitement when Sherry had discovered the hinged opening beneath the stair, but on examination it had led to nothing more exciting than the small storage space they had just examined.

"Damn!" Sherry sank into an upholstered settee by the registration desk, defeated. "I really thought there might be some connection between the hotel and whoever is hiding out up on the mountain, especially after Coolidge mentioned an escape tunnel for the casino and speakeasy."

Kelly grinned and poured her a cup of coffee from the pot sitting on the desk. "That would have been a little too convenient," he said, handing it to her. "If there really is somebody up there, they're probably holed up in a cave, which means we're going to have to find them the hard way."

She sipped her coffee, waiting until he had fixed himself a cup and settled on a chair with clawed feet. "Yes, how are we going to manage that, by the way?" she asked. "You mentioned this mysterious equipment that's arriving in the morning, but you haven't said just what it does."

"It's classified." He smiled. "What you'd call spook gear. The CIA developed it during Vietnam to detect underground bunkers being used by the enemy. With any luck it will tell us which of those holes you can see on the side of the mountain are really cave entrances and which are just surface depressions. Ought to save us a whole lot of climbing."

"And if we do discover a cave?"

"There's some specialized sound-detection equipment we can use to determine whether there's anybody moving around inside."

"I'm impressed," she said. "So, say we find a cave and there is somebody inside. What then?"

He shrugged and stared into his coffee cup. "I don't know yet. I'm making this up as we go along."

She watched him drink his coffee. "Can I ask you a personal question?" she asked.

He looked up, surprised. "How personal?"

"Frankly, I just can't get used to the idea that you make your living killing people," she said.

"Well, I've never quite gotten used to it myself. But it's probably not anything like you imagine." He searched for the right words with which to verbalize what he did. The best he could come up with was, "It's impersonal. By that I mean, that I always know who they are and what they've done, but I don't *know* them."

"But *why* do you do it?" she persisted.

Kelly shrugged. "Because somebody has to."

"But why you?" Her voice was soft, questioning.

He got to his feet and crossed the room to look out onto the veranda. The moon was coming up, casting an aura around his body. "I'm good at it," he answered defensively.

He turned to face her and she saw something cold and alien flicker just behind his eyes. "In fact, I'm the very best there is."

"Was it because of what happened in Bremerton . . . with your girlfriend? . . ."

"Her name was Diana. Diana Casey."

"Because of what happened to . . . Diana?"

Kelly turned back to the window. His voice was distant. "I suppose that was how it started."

He felt her touch his shoulder and looked down to see her standing beside him.

"You shouldn't have let it ruin your whole life, Chris," she whispered.

He nodded. "I know."

Sherry turned to him and he suddenly pulled her close. Electricity seemed to race along his body, sensitizing his every nerve ending as her lips touched his. He felt her pressing closer, the contours of her body pushing urgently against his. The kiss was long and lingering. He finally pulled away, surprised to see the hot tears running down her cheeks.

"What's wrong?" he breathed.

"You think he did it, don't you? The Phantom?"

"Yes."

"You're going to kill him, aren't you?"

"If I can find him."

"Chris, don't. Let's call in the police and tell them what we know. They'll find him."

"Maybe."

She stepped away from him, gazing up into the hard mask that his face had become. "Dammit, Chris, you just told me it was *never* personal."

"I lied," he said. "It's always personal."

"You're going to end up following this lunatic into some dark hole and getting yourself killed." she said quietly.

He stood rooted to the spot, stunned by her unexpected outburst. "That would really bother you a lot," he said slowly. It was not a question.

She turned and stared out through the French doors. "Yes, it would."

He stared at her, genuinely confused. "Why?"

Sherry rolled her eyes to the ceiling. "Just forget it, okay?"

He reached for her but she snatched the flashlight from his hand and pounded up the stairs, leaving him alone in the moonlit lobby.

Johnny stood stock-still beside the secret entrance to the hotel, listening to the sounds of feet hurrying up the lobby staircase.

He was very good at standing still, able to wait silently even for hours, waiting for danger to pass him by, for prey to step within his circle.

Moments earlier he had been walking down the long underground service corridor beneath the hotel when he had heard the murmur of voices overhead, the sudden rise and fall of the woman's voice making it seem as though they were arguing.

His florid face turned a deeper shade of red at the thought of the intruders who had taken over his hotel.

His place.

He had had to drive and walk for miles because of them; was forced to work without proper light or space. Even now, their meddling was forcing him to put poor little Marilyn in the living room with Betty and Veronica and the others before she was ready.

Johnny silently knelt on the buckling green linoleum and touched the inert form he had quietly laid there when he had first heard the voices. The girl's startled blue eyes stared up at him in the glow of his light.

Sighing unhappily, Johnny lifted the girl and carried her away into the darkness. He just knew she was not going to like being with the other girls.

Not yet.

It occurred to him that he would soon have to return to the hotel and kill the intruders. He had to go back up there to get his treasure box anyway.

Kelly had stood at the French doors, watching the moonlight on the lake for several minutes after Sherry's hurried departure, his mind reeling with the implications of her sudden revelation. He still wasn't sure how he was going to deal with the unexpected turn of events, but he knew that the first step was an apology. He wanted to explain to her that finding Diana's murderer, perhaps even learning what had happened to his first and only love, was the one thing in the world that could free him to pursue a normal life.

He found another candle on the desk, lit it, and climbed the broad staircase to the second-floor landing.

The door to the bathroom at the end of the long hallway stood slightly ajar, the glow of candlelight flickering eerily out onto the polished floorboards through clouds of steam. Kelly heard the sound of running water, assuming that Sherry had decided to take a bath. Although the partially restored upper floor had no electricity, there was no shortage of hot water from the big boiler in the kitchen.

Deciding to confront her when she finished, he had placed his hand on the knob of his door to enter when Sherry stepped into the hallway from the room next door. She was carrying his flashlight and wearing a terry robe.

"I lit the candle in your room," she said in a small voice.

"Thanks . . ." The words he had intended to say were there, but he couldn't seem to get them out.

She smiled uncertainly, looking down at her robe. "I thought I'd get cleaned up a little."

"Look, about what just happened downstairs—"

She touched her fingers to his lips. "You don't have to explain. I think I was . . . assuming a little too much."

Her touch tingled against his skin. Clasping her hand in his, he shook his head. "Oh, no," he said. "No, you weren't." He pressed her hand to his lips, kissing her fingertips. "I just never dreamed it would . . . Hell, I'm not very good at saying things." He smiled and started over again. "I like being with you. Like it very much."

The sound of running water down the hall seemed suddenly very loud. He heard it beginning to splash onto the floor as he placed his arms around her and kissed her.

"Don't worry," she whispered when their lips parted. "We'll find him tomorrow and put your poor ghost to rest at last."

It was dark.

Tracy struggled to turn herself over on the smelly sofa and peered into the Pine-Sol-smelling room where the fat man had left her. A thin sliver of light shone beneath the door of the adjoining room and she could hear him in there, talking to someone.

He had carried her into the room some minutes earlier, following a long walk. She had regained consciousness sometime during the first part of that walk—they were still in the forest then—watching with frightened eyes as he had approached a solid screen of black foliage, afraid he would dump her there in the woods to die.

Instead, he had edged past the bushes, stepping into a crumbling doorway hollowed out of the rock. Taking an old-fashioned miner's hat from a hook on the rough wall, he had lit its lamp and carried her down a winding flight of steps into a dark underground space of echoing footsteps.

Much later, they had passed open doorways, the light from his headlamp briefly illuminating a jumbled roomful of tables and chairs, another filled with rusting and broken slot machines. She had pretended to be unconscious, looking at everything through hooded eyelids, trying to memorize the way back. Then he had suddenly stopped, at the foot of a narrow stairwell lined with tattered carpet, to listen.

And she had heard the voices coming from somewhere above.

He had caught her looking then, and she was afraid he would be angry. But he had simply carried her into this small room and dumped her on the sofa before disappearing into the next room and closing the door behind him.

Now, as her eyes grew accustomed to the dim light she could see that the room was filled with figures. Sitting in the darkness in chairs or arranged against the wall. She counted five in all. Their eyes glittered in the dim light leaking beneath the door. At first she had thought they were people, but the lack of movement convinced her they must be department-store dummies.

The fat man was totally insane.

She knew that now.

Tracy closed her eyes and waited, praying he would leave the room and go away. He had been in a hurry when he had bound her again after catching her on the road and she prayed she could get her hands free once more.

If only he would go away.

She heard the sound of running water some-where far away and imagined she was on Daisy Vandeveer's father's yacht in the Mediterranean.

*　*　*

Johnny was ready.

With Marilyn safe in the living room, he was finally free to do the things he needed to do before he could prepare her.

He had been sitting on the bed in the sleeping area, going over his plans with LaVerne and Shirley. Diana was staring at him from the corner, her eyes filled with hatred, but he didn't care. He had remembered everything and now he had only to go and do it.

Smiling vacantly, he stood and kissed the girls. They all giggled happily, offering their congratulations on his having found Marilyn at last, and promising to treat her just like a little sister.

All except Diana.

She glared at him and refused to speak.

Well, he didn't care anymore. He had a new girl now. Even prettier than Diana. Walking to the door, he turned out the light and padded through the living room. He stopped at the sofa and leaned over Marilyn.

Asleep.

Or pretending to be asleep.

Johnny ran a thick hand up between her thighs and pinched her. He giggled at the small whimper of terror from behind her gag. "Y-you be good!" He laughed and left the room, bolting the door behind him.

*　*　*

Neither of them had meant for it to happen like this, the lingering kiss in the hallway, her body pressing urgently against his. . . . At some point her robe had come open, his hands running over her round buttocks, pulling her tight against him.

They had made love the first time in the huge iron bathtub, the steaming water and candle-light imparting a sense of unreality to their unbridled coupling. Later, she had lain back happily in his arms, feeling his nakedness against her back as his strong hands had gently soaped her breasts. Later still, their skin red and glowing from too long in the hot water, he had carried her down the unlit corridor to his room.

They lay across his big soft bed in the moon-light and made love again, this time slowly, lingering on the edge of pleasure until the can-dle on his bureau had guttered away to nothing and gone out.

"You're not sorry, are you?" Her voice was small and husky in his ear.

He shook his head slowly from side to side. "I thought I had lost . . . this feeling forever." He stroked her damp hair. "What about you?"

She smiled in the dark. "I think this is the first time I've ever had . . . *this* feeling." She twisted her head around to look up at his silhouette. "Chris, what about Diana?"

He was silent for a long moment. "Diana is gone," he finally answered.

"But you loved her so much."

He nodded and she thought she heard his breath catch in his throat. "Yes." He kissed the top of her head. "And I still want the son of a bitch who killed her. Can you understand why?"

She snuggled closer, working her chin into the soft hollow of his neck. "Yes. For what he did to both of you, and to Sonny and Shelly."

"And for all the others, too," he said, "and the ones still to come. If they did get him—the police—chances are good that he'd never even stand trial. You know that, don't you?"

She nodded.

"I can't, won't, take that risk."

"Do you hate him?"

He shook his head. "No. I just want to guarantee that he'll never have the chance to do it again."

She squeezed his hand. "Don't worry," she whispered, "we'll get him."

He was sleeping soundly when he felt the presence beside the bed.

"Chris?" A whisper like the wind through the trees.

He looked up to see Diana standing near the window. She was looking pointedly at Sherry, who was snuggled up on the pillow beside him, her tangle of blond hair splayed across his shoulder. He followed Diana's gaze to the sleeping woman, feeling the guilt building within him.

"No, Chris." Diana was shaking her head slowly back and forth, a hint of a smile playing at the corners of her perfect mouth. "I'm glad," she whispered.

"Oh, Christ, Diana." He sobbed, realizing that it still hurt to speak her name.

"I only wish it were me," she said. Her form was slowly fading into the moonlight across the sill.

"Be careful, Chris," she whispered. "He knows you're here. He's insane, but clever. Oh, so very clever."

She was nearly gone now, a hint of lingering phosphorescence by the casement.

"Diana, wait! Where is he?"

Gone now, only the faintest echo of her voice fading away in the night.

"Nearby, Chris. Too near . . ."

Kelly sat up, sweating. He rubbed his eyes, gazing at the empty window casement, trying to remember at precisely what point he had awakened.

False dawn.

Johnny looked out through the windshield of the old pickup and saw the first glimmerings of light in the eastern sky as he pulled into the deserted alleyway. The drive had taken far longer than he had anticipated, night construction work on the interstate outside of Trenton slowing traffic to a one-lane crawl for miles.

He had to hurry.

Stepping out of the cab and stretching his massive body, he crushed his cigarette and hefted the crowbar he'd pulled from behind the seat. The looming bulk of the old brick building in a run-down industrial section of the city towered over him. Unconcerned about the possibility of being spotted, he climbed up onto the dimly lit loading dock, calmly smashed the single bulb in its overhead fixture, and inserted the crowbar beneath the hasp of the padlocked metal door. He had done this before and knew that the Northeast Prosthetics Company didn't bother to keep a watchman on the payroll. After all, nobody would bother to steal artificial eyes.

Well, almost nobody.

The cheap lock snapped under the pressure of the crowbar and Johnny stepped inside. Switching on a small penlight, he walked straight through the polishing and grinding rooms and stepped into the small display area. Hundreds of pairs of beautiful eyes looked up at him from velvet-lined cases ranked along the wall.

He began examining them carefully, searching for one special pair the exact color of Lake Lazarus beneath a summer sky.

BOOK THREE

Seek and Destroy

CHAPTER 1

Logistics

THE twisting secondary road leading down the mountain toward Bremerton kept Kelly's attention focused on his driving.

It was early Sunday morning and there was no other traffic as he guided Sherry's Mustang around curves and through short straightaways shaded by stands of laurel and mountain alder. The car's light sports suspension and the cool morning air combined to make the drive enjoyable and he realized that he hadn't felt so purposeful in years.

He had left Sherry propped among the pillows of the big four-poster in his room, sipping a cup of the bitter coffee he had managed to brew atop the balky kitchen range.

He had wanted her to come with him, uneasy at the prospect of leaving her alone at the south end of the lake for even a short time with the killer loose. She had, of course, pooh-poohed his sudden concern. She was fully armed and perfectly capable of taking care of herself, thank you very much. Besides, she had added, there were a few things she needed to do that would delay their starting out for the waterfall if she went along. He had reluctantly left, after extracting a promise not to let anyone into the hotel until he returned.

The plan was for her to shower and throw together something for breakfast while he drove to the airport to pick up Blackstone's Federal Express shipment. They would map out their strategy for setting up the detection equipment while they ate, then make an oblique approach to the area around the waterfall to begin an electronic analysis of the likely cave entrances they had spotted the previous day.

Kelly touched the responsive brakes and notched the shifter down into third gear, slowing for the sweeping curve ahead. The Mustang glided smoothly into the turn and shot onto the steep downgrade on the other side. He shifted again and allowed himself a self-satisfied grin. For the first time in as long as he could remember, he was looking forward to the future. Together, he and Sherry would find the man who had killed Sonny . . . and perhaps Diana, too. After that, well, he had plans.

His smile faded as he recalled the vivid dream of the previous night. Diana had smiled at him, happy he had found someone new at last. He wondered if that was his own subconscious's not-so-subtle way of finally absolving him of his guilt. He stretched his shoulders and smiled again. Wherever it had come from, the dream seemed to have lifted a great weight from his soul and he felt good.

After today he would fly back to Washington to resign from Harvest. Blackstone would present a dozen good reasons why he shouldn't, of course. Probably, the old man would try to make him feel guilty. Well, Chris decided, it was too late for guilt. He was sick of it. He'd done his bit for the world, right or wrong, and now he planned to catch up on the rest of his life. The first thing he would do after resigning would be to put the Virginia condo on the market and move up to Lake Lazarus to see if he could help Shelly and the boys make a go of the hotel. If he was damned lucky, he figured—luckier than he had any right to be—Sherry Mahan would be a part of his new life.

Luck.

He remembered Diana's final words from his dream—another piece of advice from his subconscious, and a damn good one at that—the killer in the forest was clever. What had happened to Sonny proved that the maniac would not hesitate to kill him, and Sherry, too.

"Be careful," she had warned.

"Damn right!" He said the words aloud, realizing that the prospect of the new life taking shape in his future would make him more careful than he had ever been. For now he had something to lose.

The road leveled ahead as the Mustang plunged into a dark corridor of towering pines. Kelly eased the wheel slightly to the left, allowing plenty of room for the old pickup truck that was approaching from the opposite direction. It flashed past him in the gloom cast by the interlocking branches of the trees, affording him a momentary glimpse of a very fat man at the wheel.

He was wearing a red baseball cap and drinking orange soda from a can.

There was faded writing forming the word *taxidermy* in a half circle about a deer's head on the door of the old truck, and a green wooden box in the back.

Kelly frowned slightly as the Mustang shot out into the bright morning sunlight beyond the grove of pines. He glanced into the rearview mirror for another look, but the old truck was already gone and he shrugged off the nagging feeling that there was something he should have remembered about it. The fat guy behind the wheel had looked harmless enough.

Johnny was tired but happy.

His trip to Trenton had been a success. The pair of glass eyes clicking softly together in his shirt pocket were just perfect. He couldn't wait to show them to Marilyn, to explain how beautiful they were going to make her.

He belched loudly, his stomach full at last, the result of the leisurely breakfast he had just enjoyed at a bustling truck stop along the interstate. He grinned crookedly, remembering how the wrinkled waitress with the big hanky folded into a corsage on her massive bosom had fussed over him, bringing him extra syrup for his double order of pancakes and marveling at his ability to consume half a dozen eggs and a dozen slices of crisp bacon.

The woman had brushed against him several times as she had leaned over the Formica counter to refill his glass of orange soda, allowing her sagging boobs to touch his naked forearm.

Johnny had wanted to laugh right out loud at her; to tell her that he didn't need any baggy old women with too much paint on their faces to give him a thrill. Not when he had a secret place filled with beautiful girls who would do anything he wanted whenever he felt like it; girls prettier than the ones on TV.

Of course, he had said nothing, simply grinning at the stupid old woman and holding out his glass for all the free refills of orange soda she was giving.

The truck bounced over a rough spot in the road and he glanced back through the dirty rear window to be sure the box was securely locked. In it were the other things he would need to make Marilyn good. He focused his eyes on the road again, mentally reviewing the contents of the other girls' closet. He would have to find something for the new girl to wear since she had insisted on ruining her pretty outfit with the red high-heeled shoes.

A good thing she hadn't hurt herself with all of that running-away nonsense, he reflected. Now, that would have been a real shame. As it was, Johnny was going to have to give her a good scrubbing before he could prepare her. He frowned, wondering how he was going to manage that. There was no running water in the hideaway.

Sherry Mahan stood beneath the stinging spray of a hot shower, letting the steam and the pounding of the water drive the tension from her body.

She was still having a hard time coming to grips with the sheer magnitude of the passion that had been unleashed within her by Chris Kelly and it seemed, as she soaped the tender areas around her breasts and thighs, that she could still feel his hands upon her, gentle and persistent.

Closing her eyes, she squeezed shampoo into her hair from a plastic bottle and massaged it into a thick lather. She realized now that she had found herself incredibly attracted to Kelly from the first moment she had laid eyes on him, something in his solemn gaze and quiet manner drawing her inexorably to him. Hell, she had deliberately set out to bed him last night, excited by the taut, muscled chest and firm buttocks she couldn't help glimpsing when he had stripped to enter the pool below the waterfall. She had already known that he was similarly aroused by the sight of her body and had figured they would have great sex together.

And they had.

But then the other thing had happened, the feeling of not wanting him to let her go when it was over. The warm, flushed sensation of lying next to him and thinking about the next time, and the next.

There was a vulnerability to Chris Kelly that belied both his occupation and his history, a soft warm space within him that she knew only she could properly fill. Sherry had been truly and deeply in love with only one other man in her life—not, unfortunately, the preening, macho actor she had married and then divorced in Los Angeles. She had foolishly allowed that first love to wither and die without ever doing anything about it, more intent at the time on getting her degree in criminal psychology and beginning her career than in marrying. Now she vowed not to make the same mistake again. God knew Chris Kelly had his demons—the haunting memory of the girl so brutally taken from him, a life spent executing other men. If he would let her, she would help him conquer those demons, and together they would find real happiness.

She rinsed the shampoo out of her hair and reached through the opening in the plastic shower curtain for the towel hanging on the rack beside the tub. A draft of cold air blew onto her arm from the opened bathroom door and she opened her eyes to see the haggard figure standing there, watching her through red-rimmed eyes.

*   *   *

Blackstone's shipment was not on the plane.

The harried Federal Express clerk, still grumbling at having been called in on a Sunday to handle the special delivery, was not amused. He stood behind the counter in the back of Bremerton Airport's tiny freight terminal punching numbers into his computer and frowning.

"Best I can tell," he finally said without taking his eyes off the glowing screen, "is that the package was routed from Washington National to JFK. It should have gone on the seven-thirty flight from JFK to here. . . ."

Kelly drummed his fingers on the counter. "It should have, but did it?"

The clerk punched more numbers into the keyboard. "Well, it says here that it did, which probably means . . ." He punched up a few more numbers. " . . . that it wasn't taken off the flight when it arrived here." He peered at the screen and winced. "I'd say it's in Pittsburgh by now . . . or Cleveland."

"Shit!" Kelly still couldn't believe that Harvest relied on commercial shippers to move their critical equipment around the world.

The clerk leaned over his terminal again. "I'll call ahead and have them reroute it," he said. "We can have it back here by noon."

"Great," said Kelly. "I drove all the way down here from Lake Lazarus."

"No problem," said the clerk. "We'll send it up to you."

Kelly rubbed his chin thoughtfully. The only reason he had driven to the airport to pick up the gear was to avoid the activity of a delivery to the hotel. "That's okay," he said, resigning himself to the wait. "I'd just as soon not have you send a truck up there."

"Oh, we don't have a truck on today," said the clerk. "I'd just send it on up by taxi. Of course, it'd cost you extra for the fare. . . ."

Kelly wasn't listening to him. He was remembering the old beat-up truck that had passed him on the mountain road, the one with the word *taxidermy* hand-lettered on the door . . . the same truck Sonny Lasco had found parked in the shed by the hotel the weekend the furniture had gone missing. He turned and pounded out through the swinging door.

"Hey," called the clerk, "what do you want me to do with your shipment when it gets in?"

Kelly turned and hollered at him from the loading dock. "Go ahead and send it up to the old hotel at the south end of the lake as soon as it arrives!"

"By taxi?" yelled the clerk.

Kelly nodded and dived into the Mustang.

Although he had nothing concrete on which to base it, there was a sick feeling deep in the pit of his stomach.

"I'm sorry I frightened you. I just couldn't sit down there doing nothing." Shelly Lasco sat on the edge of Sherry's bed, sniffling into a handkerchief.

"Well, you only scared me out of a year's growth,"

Sherry said. She finished toweling her hair dry, ran a brush though it before the mirror, and pulled on a T-shirt before turning to face her friend. "You really shouldn't have come up here, Shelly," she said worriedly. She wasn't sure exactly how long Chris had been gone, but she didn't want to run the risk of him arriving back at the hotel with the specialized gear while Shelly was still there.

Shelly dabbed at her eyes. "I know," she said. "The boys are probably going to be frantic when they come home and find me gone."

"Where are the boys this morning?" Sherry was as surprised to learn that Shelly had come all the way up to the lake alone as she had been to see her standing there in the bathroom doorway a few minutes earlier.

"I sent them to church . . . to say a prayer for their dad." She hesitated. "I told them I was going to sleep in this morning."

"Well, I'm driving you right back home," insisted Sherry. "Chris will be very upset if he finds you here when he gets back. He's been very worried about you."

"I can't believe I missed him." Shelly looked around the room in confusion. "Why did you say he went to the airport?"

"He had to pick up some papers to do with his work," she lied. "I guess he took off to come up here in such a hurry that he left some things in Washington that needed to be signed."

"Oh." Shelly seemed satisfied with the explanation.

"Okay, now, here's what we're going to do.

We're going to leave Chris a note, and I'm going to drive you back to Bremerton and put you to bed. Chris can drive back down and get me later and then you can see him, too." Sherry didn't like the plan at all, but it was the best she could come up with on short notice. She searched the top of her dresser for a pencil and paper, remembered she had seen one in the lacquered lost-and-found box, a tiny gold mechanical thing attached to a leatherette notebook. Dumping the box's contents onto the dresser, she found the book and pencil and began scribbling a hurried note to Kelly.

Shelly stopped sniffling and got to her feet. "This is silly," she said. "It was stupid of me to come up here without telling anyone. There's no need for you to take me. I'm perfectly capable of driving myself back home."

"Oh, no you're not," said Sherry. She folded the note, then straightened and turned to face her friend. "All we need right now is for you to run off that road all pumped full of Valium, or whatever they've been giving you. I'm driving you home and that's final."

Shelly stared past her. Her shoulders suddenly began to heave and Sherry put her arms around her, patting her back comfortingly. "Come on, now. It's going to be all right. Would you like some coffee first?"

The older woman suddenly pulled free and jerked her head impatiently from side to side.

Sherry looked worriedly at her, confused by the strange behavior. "Shelly, are you all right?"

Shelly pointed a trembling finger at the collection of trinkets scattered across the top of the dresser. "Where did you get that?" she mumbled in a zombielike monotone.

Sherry half turned to see what she was pointing at. "The box? I found it in the kitchen, I—"

Brushing her aside, Shelly snatched the blackened silver bracelet from the dresser and held it up into the light. "No," she whispered, "not the box. This!"

"The bracelet? It was in the box with the other things. Why, Shelly, what's wrong?"

Shelly's eyes wore a stunned glaze as she turned the shining hoop over and over in her hands. "I helped him pick this out for her," she muttered. "She was wearing it that night."

Sherry was growing seriously concerned about her friend. She was convinced now that Shelly was having some sort of delayed breakdown as the result of the previous weeks' stresses. "I don't understand," she began gently. "Who was wearing it, Shelly?"

Shelly's eyes darted wildly around the room. "Her!" she whispered. "Diana. Chris gave it to her for Christmas . . . that night. The night she disappeared."

"It can't be the same one," said Sherry. "I mean, maybe it just looks like it. . . ."

A strange, gurgling laugh bubbled up out of Shelly's throat. She shook her head and ran her tongue across the entwined metal hearts, then rubbed the bracelet vigorously on the hem of her skirt. "No. It was this exact one," she said with growing horror in her voice. "See!"

She raised the bracelet to the powerful spill of sunlight streaming in through the window. The spidery engraving shone black against the silver hearts.

Sherry stared at the bracelet. "It's true," she breathed, "it's really true!"

Her bereaved friend grabbed her by the arm and jerked her around to stare into her eyes. "What's true, Sherry? How did Diana's bracelet get here?"

Sherry opened her dresser drawer and removed the small automatic pistol. "Come on," she said, "we're getting out of this place right now. I'll explain in the car."

"You'll explain now, goddammit!" Shelly's voice rose to a screech. "Where did this bracelet come from and what has it got to do with my Sonny's disappearance?"

"Shelly, please." Sherry looked uneasily over her shoulder. The bracelet conclusively proved the killer had access to the old hotel. Access, hell, it was probably his *turf,* the box filled with jewelry a testament to the number of victims he had taken.

Her mind jumped back to the criminology refresher course she'd taken at Penn State the previous year. There had been a lecture on the psychology of serial killers—they often kept mementos taken from their victims.

The lost-and-found box.

How could she have been so stupid?

The Phantom had been right here all along. He might be just outside the door now, listening. Lurking in the darkened hallway . . .

"Honey," she said, keeping her voice low and raising the small pistol so that it was pointing at the ceiling, ready for an instant response to any threat, "we've got to leave here right now. Very quickly and very quietly."

Shelly seemed to deflate before her eyes. She looked at her like a lost child. "What's going on, Sherry? Please tell me."

"We—Chris and I—think the man who . . . killed Sonny may still be around here," she said. "I didn't connect the bracelet with him earlier, but the fact that I found it in the hotel proves he's been in here. That's why we have to leave. Do you see?"

Shelly nodded her understanding. "What if Chris comes back?" she whispered.

Sherry thought for a moment. "We'll wait out at the end of the road for him," she said. "That's the only way in here." She crumpled the note she had just written and tossed it onto the dresser top and the two women hurried out of the room together.

CHAPTER 2

Missing Persons

KELLY fumed behind the wheel of the Mustang. Halfway up the mountain road from Bremerton a carload of rollicking teenagers had attempted to pass a motor home chugging up a steep, narrow grade with a fishing boat in tow. The resulting crash had left three of the kids stretched out beside the shoulder with injuries ranging in severity from a badly broken arm to a profusely bleeding scalp wound. The heavy fishing rig had jackknifed over the motor home, tipping the clumsy vehicle onto its side and blocking the road in both directions with the wreckage and half its contents.

Arriving on the scene moments after the accident, Kelly had had no choice but to stop the car and tend to the victims' most urgent needs. He sent the next car to arrive back down the hill to find a phone and call for police and an ambulance while he busied himself applying a pressure bandage to the head of the bleeding teenager, showing one of the uninjured kids how to hold it in place. After getting the others off the road and making them as comfortable as possible while assuring himself that none of their injuries was life threatening, he turned his attention to the motor home.

Its driver, a crusty old retiree in a pair of faded jungle fatigues, seemed to be merely shaken by the accident. The volume and quality of his language bespoke his former occupation as a marine gunnery sergeant. "Little fuckers," he hollered, glaring back down the road at the battered teenagers, "I'll have every one of your asses for this!"

"Take it easy, Gunny," said Kelly, dropping into the old Corps lingo. "I saw the whole thing. You and your lawyers are going to end up owning their daddies' insurance policies."

The old man grinned viciously, then stepped back to scrutinize Kelly. "You talk the talk, sonny, do you walk the walk?" he asked, paraphrasing the familiar line from every hard-core marine's favorite movie, *Full Metal Jacket.*

Kelly laughed. "Parris Island, '67," he said. "Former Corporal Christopher J. Kelly, at your service."

"Out-fucking-standing, Corporal!" yelled the old coot, clapping him on the back so hard it nearly knocked Kelly over. "You willin' to testify that them little pogies damn near killed me tryin' to pass on a blind curve?"

Kelly nodded and was rewarded with another deadly backslap.

"I won't forget this, Corporal."

Kelly looked worriedly down the mountain. A siren wailed faintly in the distance and a long line of cars was piling up behind the wreck. He turned back to the old marine, who was grimly surveying the battered remains of his pride and joy. "The thing is, Gunny," he began, "I have this little problem up at the lake, and I thought you might give me a little hand."

"Name it, lad."

Kelly pointed to the two things he wanted to borrow.

A loud hissing noise.

Soap and hot water.

Tracy smelled the scent of the soap first, a cheap flowery perfume of some supermarket brand she wouldn't be caught dead using.

Then more water splashed into her face and she choked, realizing as her eyes flew open that she was no longer gagged.

An intense glare of white light flooded down on her from above and she squinted as a big hand appeared from the darkness surrounding the light. A big hand holding a dripping sponge. She felt water dribbling onto her chest and looked down at her body.

She was completely naked, stretched out on a rough wooden table. Inch-thick eyebolts had been screwed into the tabletop and through each of these had been wound a stout leather strap. The straps were attached to her wrists and ankles.

She screamed, an ear-splitting shriek that echoed off the thick stone walls.

The sponge was pressed into her face, cutting off the scream and suffocating her. She looked beyond the light with terrified eyes and saw the fat man grinning down at her from behind a stained leather apron.

"B-bad girl!" he admonished, wagging his head. A cloud of steam issued from between his lips and she realized that it was freezing in the room.

He lifted the sponge from her face, holding it poised just above her nose, and she gasped greedily in the frigid air, gathering her strength to scream again. The fat man shook his head slightly and she decided not to scream.

The fat man seemed pleased. Dropping the sponge into a container somewhere beyond the range of her vision, he disappeared from view.

Tracy craned her neck, trying to see past the bright overhead light. She made out the shadowy forms of two people sitting against the far wall. Unblinking eyes stared back at her from the darkness.

The man reappeared, leaning over her. She cringed away from his fetid breath, arching her body against the straps. Ignoring her struggles, he slipped a gentle hand beneath her head, raising it and tilting a metal container to her lips. She gagged and choked as the sickly sweet taste of warm orange soda filled her mouth. He waited patiently until she regained her breath, then lifted her head again. She sucked greedily at the nauseating liquid, realizing that it had been a whole day since she had eaten or drunk.

The fat man let her drink her fill, then disappeared from view again. She heard the crackle of cellophane being ripped and he was back, holding a slender yellow cake between his thick, spatulate fingers. She laughed hysterically, then opened her mouth to receive the food. The fact that he was taking the time to feed her was hopeful. It meant he did not plan to kill her.

Not right away.

When the man had fed her another Twinkie he retrieved his sponge and went to work washing her body. He cooed and murmured over her as he worked, stopping from time to time to stroke her skin, gently squeezing her red nipples in wonder. Tracy fell back against the wooden table and closed her eyes, feeling the dirt and mud being sponged gently away from her, the hot, soothing suds running down her thighs, pooling beneath her buttocks.

Her mind was numb with terror at what might follow next and she tried to think about how to react when, inevitably, he at last decided to rape her. Should she cooperate, as some of her friends had speculated? She was certainly in no position to fight him off. Perhaps she should beg him for mercy. She had heard that some rapists got off on that. That it was what they wanted.

Maybe she should scream at him, demand that he release her—

The washing stopped.

She opened her eyes and looked up to see him smiling down at her. He began to pat her body dry with a fluffy pink towel. She wanted to scream: scream and never stop screaming. Instead, she looked into his eyes and opened her mouth to speak. "My father is very rich," she said in a tremulous voice. "He'll pay you anything you want if you'll just take me home."

He had stopped drying her and was watching her curiously, his big misshapen head tilted to one side to catch her words above the hissing of the lamp.

"I promise," she continued, "that no one will try to come after you or call the police . . . or anything."

He seemed to consider this information for a moment, then resumed drying her, running the towel between her thighs and patting the soft mound of golden pubic hair. "M-My name's . . . J-Johnny," he said. His beady eyes darted to hers, waiting for her reaction.

Tracy swallowed hard, tasting the sticky remains of the Twinkie in the back of her throat. She raised her head to look up at him and forced herself to smile. "Hello . . . Johnny. My name is Tracy."

Johnny's face twisted into an insane grin and he giggled through hideous teeth. "N-No," he said as though it were the most hilarious joke in the world. "Y-Your n-name is . . . M-M-Marilyn."

Tracy screamed as his cruel fingers snatched a lock of pubic hair and wrenched it.

His bloated features hardened into a hideous mask as he leered down at her, blowing his stinking breath at her.

She could feel the hatred in his gravelly voice as he screamed the words, drowning out her own scream. "Y-Your n-name is Marilyn . . . and you're b-bad!"

CHAPTER 3

Force Reconnaissance

WIND and speed and noise.

Kelly gunned the old marine's rugged trail bike up the last steep grade leading to the lake. The crumbling tarmac road circling past the campground stretched empty ahead and he leaned forward, urging more speed from the heavy machine.

It had taken an additional twenty minutes to free the bike from the tangle of fishing tackle and the smashed rack that had secured it to the back of the overturned motor home: another ten minutes to rip off the twisted rear fender and start the flooded engine. The first state police car was just making its way past the stalled line of cars behind the Mustang as he had squeezed the motorcycle through the narrow gap between the mountainside and the motor home and rocketed away up the mountain.

He had been tempted to identify himself to the cops at that point, but he knew that more precious time would be wasted answering questions, confirming he was who and what he said he was, and still the road would be blocked. And even if he had gone through all of that, he still had nothing more concrete to offer the authorities than a bad feeling.

A very bad feeling.

The borrowed motorcycle flew down the rough road with Kelly clinging to it. The hard, comforting weight of the old man's hunting rifle, a modified M14 with a twelve-power scope, pressed against his back as he reviewed the scanty information he possessed.

One, Sonny was dead, murdered by a person or persons unknown and his body cleverly hidden below the waterfall at the south end of the lake.

Two, several other people had disappeared at the south end of the lake in previous years, just like Sonny—a good indicator that the same person or persons were responsible for their deaths as well.

Three, a suspected serial killer known as the Phantom had been abducting young women for years in a wide geographical area, of which the lake was the center. They, too, had all disappeared without a trace.

Four, the old pickup truck was undoubtedly the same one that Sonny and his boys had seen after someone had been in the hotel removing furniture and other items! The truck that Kelly had spotted heading up the mountain to the lake more than three hours ago . . .

Taken together, it was more than enough to justify what he was doing now. He wanted Sherry out of the old hotel as quickly as possible. Once she was out of immediate danger, they could go down the mountain to retrieve her car and plan their next move.

The road curved to his left, breaking out of the trees and running along the shore of the lake for a short distance. He could see the turrets of the Summerland Hotel shining in the early afternoon sun.

Looking placid and harmless.

Trees intervened to block his view again and he leaned into a sharp curve, speeding up the same section of road he had walked after being dropped off by the helicopter two nights earlier. A crumbling building appeared among the trees; an old storage shed of some sort that he had not noticed before. He wondered at its original purpose and whether it comprised part of the hotel property—his property.

Then it was gone, lost among the thick foliage, and he could see the twin turrets at the ends of the hotel looming above the trees.

He thought briefly of that first night, and of Sherry with her candles and her sheer nightgown. He wondered if she was still holding the breakfast she'd fixed for them, and if she was going to be pissed because he was nearly two hours late.

*   *   *

Sherry lay on her side in the pitch-black room where she had come to some time earlier to discover her hands and feet professionally bound and a heavy piece of tape securing her mouth.

Her head was splitting.

She was lying on a narrow bed facing a wall of rough plaster. She tried to roll over and found that she could not. There was someone else lying beside her, she could feel the weight pressing against her back.

Shelly.

She wriggled her fingers against the other body, hoping for some answering response. She felt soft fabric over yielding flesh.

Nothing more.

It came to her then that Shelly must still be unconscious, felled no doubt by the same horrible spray that had put her out. Ether. The pungent, nauseating smell of it still lingered in her hair.

Sherry had a sudden horrible thought. What if the madman who had brought them here had given Shelly too much of the powerful anesthetic? Or gagged her too tightly? She felt as if she might vomit herself, knew it was possible to strangle. . . .

Driving the awful thought from her mind, she tried to concentrate on the predicament she had gotten them into.

Christ, she had been so damn stupid, driving Shelly's little Toyota a mile down the road from the hotel and parking there to await Chris's arrival, thinking they were safe in the bright sunshine, while the murderous fat man was patiently creeping up on the two of them from the deep woods right beside the road.

The muzzle of his rifle had slipped in through the open window, the uncompromising black tip of it touching the soft flesh behind her ear before she had even realized he was there.

Some fucking cop!

He had withdrawn the rifle from the car then, forcing her to start the engine, and walking along beside the slowly moving car with his gun trained on Shelly's head as she had backed down the road to the tumbledown shed at the edge of the hotel property. It was the shed where he'd parked his old truck, the same truck she had seen at the campground the previous day.

Johnny.

Johnny, the half-witted taxidermist.

Johnny, the serial murderer known as the Phantom.

Christ almighty!

He had led them up into the woods, prodding and nudging with the rifle as they had climbed toward the waterfall, always at their backs, his finger never off the trigger, the insane, drooling grin never absent from his face.

Crazy. Murderously crazy, with a ferretlike cunning that had left him free to roam the northeastern territory known as Phantomland, killing God knew how many innocent people for God knew how many years.

Shelly had stumbled along through the woods ahead of her like a zombie, no longer knowing or caring what was happening. She herself had lagged behind, pretending to trip over roots and branches along the steep trail, stalling for as long as possible: hoping he would give her an opening—any opening.

He never did.

The route to the waterfall was much shorter from where the truck was parked than the way she and Kelly had climbed the previous day. They had stepped into the sunny clearing by the pool less than fifteen minutes from their starting point, Johnny prodding impatiently at their backs with the rifle, directing them toward a stony wall covered with a thick screen of scrub growth. She had started to protest, been pushed rudely forward.

That was when she had seen the doorway cut directly into the side of the mountain, the steps leading down into the pitch darkness.

There had been a single instant then when she might have taken him, as he squeezed his bulk through the narrow doorway, lowering the rifle and reaching for a lantern hung on the rock wall. She had half turned, seen the demented glow in his eyes: those mad eyes, small and beady, full of cunning and animal intelligence. Go ahead, said the eyes. Try it.

Please.

She had smiled and shrugged helplessly, taking poor, silent Shelly by the arm and guiding her down the dark metal steps, their footsteps echoing hollowly in the vastness of some great subterranean space below. She would have to make her move later, when he felt more secure.

After a few minutes on the steps they had emerged into a sloping natural cavern; the floor slick and muddy beneath their feet. As they had walked, always moving downward, she had understood at last how the distant waterfall had served as the escape point for the Prohibition-era refugees from the hotel, as Coolidge had claimed. The huge cave was the conduit. The 1920s mobsters had only had to dig an entrance at either end in order to create a foolproof getaway route.

They had walked for another twenty minutes, coming finally to a door cut into the living rock of the cavern. Stepping through a short tunnel, they emerged into a long linoleum-floored corridor lined with dusty statues of naked nymphs and the potted remains of long-dead rubber plants.

The place smelled of death.

The fat man had stopped them before a closed door, ordered them to turn around.

Another chance to take him?

The shot of ether from the plastic bottle in his hand had hit her in the eyes, dropping her to her knees like an elephant she had once seen in a film about ivory poachers.

She remembered gasping for breath as the world grew suddenly dark, glimpsing Shelly's limp body sprawled on the floor beside her.

Sherry wriggled her fingers again, praying for some response from Shelly.

There was still nothing.

She listened with growing terror to the labored sound of her own breathing. A faint, foul odor, as of something too long dead, permeated the rough fabric of the dusty bedcovering against her cheek.

Somewhere, far away, she imagined she could hear someone screaming.

Kelly stopped the motorcycle just short of the portico covering the hotel entrance. Switching off the noisy engine, he pulled the heavy bike up onto its stand and stared curiously at the front door.

He had fully expected Sherry to be standing there waiting for him, her curiosity aroused by the whining racket of the approaching dirt bike.

A bird called to its mate from the trees edging the lawn. A squirrel chattered noisily from its perch atop a broken piece of statuary. The motorcycle's engine ticked quietly as hot metal cooled in the mountain air.

Before him, the silent hotel brooded in the bright afternoon sunshine, blank windows looking down on the ruined lawn. No door opened. No curious voice called out to inquire where in the hell he had been for the last three hours and why he had returned on the noisy contraption instead of in her precious Mustang.

Nothing.

Puzzled, Kelly stepped off the bike.

Something wrong, or merely his imagination?

He tried to think of a place in the hotel where the bike's approach wouldn't have been heard from at least half a mile away.

The shower.

Maybe.

Unslinging the modified M14 from his back, he inserted a fat black twenty-round magazine—the only one the old gunny had in the motor home—into the breech. He felt the loud, satisfying click as the magazine locked into place. He pulled the slide and released, glimpsing a coppery flash as the first of the metal-jacketed NATO rounds slid into the chamber.

Locked and loaded.

Safety off.

Kelly took a tentative step toward the glass front doors, then hesitated. Turning quietly on his heel, he moved in closer to the freshly painted clapboard wall and backtracked to the far end of the building. A cricket chirped among the shrubbery. An outboard motor came to life and droned monotonously at the far end of the lake.

Sweat dripped into his eyes as he made his way to the back of the hotel, stopping at each corner to sweep a clear field of fire.

He scanned the empty veranda from the shadows at the end of the building, then climbed over the railing and pressed his back to the wall. Reaching the French doors, he peered cautiously into the empty lobby. When he was satisfied that there was no one inside, he opened the nearest door and slipped inside to check out the lower floor. Rifle at the ready, he moved silently from room to room in the prescribed manner, never stepping directly into a doorway, keeping to the walls and away from the windows. It was a maneuver he had practiced a hundred times in the field and the responses were automatic.

At the end of ten minutes he had swept the entire lower floor and found himself standing at the foot of the stairs. The hollow sound of dripping water echoed faintly from the floor above.

The Bad Thing

T H E Y all thought he was stupid.

The swaggering, tough kids in school who had made fun of his pudgy body and halting speech had beaten him up nearly every day of his young life, taking his lunch money and pulling down the funny overalls his mother always made him wear and pushing him into the girls' room with hoots and jeers and obscene suggestions. And the girls, the pretty, perky Peggys and Jessicas with their tossing curls and pleated skirts, hiding their pretty mouths behind soft, fluttering porcelain hands and telling the boys how perfectly horrible and just awful they were for the things they did to poor little Johnny Skinner, while all the time he could see the little hidden sparkles of laughter in their flashing blue and green and brown eyes. The girls were even worse than the boys.

His teachers, who had once sent a note to his mother telling her that he was something they called dull normal, driving her into one of her rages that had lasted for days and days.

And all the people in the stores and diners, who always squinted at his crooked teeth and uneven haircut and bitten fingernails and talked to him as if he were a dog or something, smirking and clucking their tongues as he carefully counted out the money for bread and milk and sewing needles to be sure he had the right change so his mother wouldn't beat him when he came home.

His mother, too. Even her. Hitting him on his ears with her thick, tattered Bible and telling him it was his fault that his daddy had blown his head off and gone to burn in hell—if only he hadn't taken to drink in his despair over having such a fat, stupid, bad boy for a son it never would have happened.

Never in a million years, she said.

They all thought Johnny was stupid: all except his daddy; his daddy, who was tall and strong as a big brown tree and who had always smiled and patted him on his head and told him he was a good boy and took him for long rides on his shoulders in the forest whenever his mother was having one of her "spells" and showed him how to gut and skin animals and where to find roots you could eat that tasted just like chewy candy, and how to build an Indian lodge out of young saplings and woven willow branches, and who never, ever once talked about the bad thing, even though his mother screamed and raved and said she'd never let his daddy do it to her again and it was all he ever wanted from her even though she was a clean, decent Christian woman and had never been raised that way.

But his daddy was long gone to hell.

And, afterward, all the rest of them had teased and prodded and jeered and tortured and beaten and laughed at him until he had become a wild creature, skipping school to prowl the woods and watch the animals and dig his secret burrows, returning only when driven by hunger and the cold to the over-heated cabin where his mother still ranted and prayed and cursed him for his stupidity and uttered her dire, hellish warnings, sewing him up tight so the bad thing would never happen to him and ruin his life like it had ruined hers.

But Johnny knew he wasn't stupid.

He had learned that the bad thing still happened, even if you sewed yourself up tight with thick black thread. You couldn't help the bad thing from happening.

Especially if you were a girl. Girls were born bad.

Johnny stood swaying over the naked girl on the table. Despite the frigid air in the cold room, great greasy droplets of sweat were pouring down his flaccid cheeks, splashing onto her naked breasts and belly as he struggled to explain it all to her, to make her understand about the bad thing and how it was what made people, especially pretty girls like her, do mean, horrible things to other people—people like him. Things that made them burn in hell forever. Like his poor daddy.

He was gasping with the effort now, spurts of steam jetting from his flared nostrils as he explained about the golden star and the light that came from it, the light that you could see when you took the bad thing away.

"See?" he said, panting.

"See?"

Tracy Swanson stared at him, her gorgeous blue eyes bulging like marbles in the pale mask of her face. A long, uncontrollable tremor wracked her beautiful body as the effects of the cold room and the raving lunatic hovering above her in the glaring light plunged her into the final stages of shock.

Johnny leaned closer, the heat of his stinking breath creating the illusion of a glowing circle of blessed warmth on her right breast.

"See?" he screamed in frustration.

Tracy shook her head weakly. "P-please . . ." she pleaded, "soooo . . . c-cold!"

He stood wearily, pacing to the wooden bench where Liz and Farrah sat silently regarding the table.

"S-She don't get it," he mumbled.

They watched sympathetically as he removed the stained leather apron and unbuttoned the straps holding up his overalls. He was sure they knew how terribly tired he was, how much he hated having to show Marilyn the bad thing to make her understand.

CHAPTER 5

Trail

EMPTY.

Kelly stood at the doorway to Sherry's bedroom. Lace curtains fluttered in the light afternoon breeze. A damp towel hung drying on a rack beside the dresser.

He eyed the upended lacquer box, the scatter of cheap jewelry on the dresser top. Lowering the rifle and clicking on the safety, he sank into a chair by the bed and stared out at the wind-riffled surface of the lake. Where in the hell had she gone?

He had been through the entire hotel, having thoroughly and methodically swept the second floor, then the one above it as well as the turrets at either end; a slow, nerve-wracking process that had entailed opening dozens of doors, probing into dusty rooms filled with nothing more sinister than peeling wallpaper and shrouded furniture.

In the end, he had returned to the small section of the second floor the two of them had shared, stepping into the bathroom and wondering at the strange slop of water on the floor—strange, because the previous night, even in the heat of their passion, she had insisted on mopping up the overflow from the neglected tub before they had moved to the bedroom, afraid of ruining the newly tiled floor.

He looked around her bedroom again. A sudden gust of air blew the curtains harder, swirling into the room and tumbling a crumpled ball of paper onto the floor from the dresser. He stood and followed it to the wall, stooping to pick it up.

Crossing back to the window, he laid the rifle across the chair and smoothed the tiny sheet of lined paper.

Chris,
Shelly showed up in a state right after you left. I'm driving her back home. Will you pick me up there? I'll explain.
Love, Sher

"Jesus!" Kelly exhaled and dropped onto the bed. The horrifying visions of Sherry in the clutches of the faceless killer dissipated like storm clouds. He looked at the old gunny's rifle, feeling incredibly stupid for having assumed the worst when the explanation was so patently simple. The only good thing was that Sherry hadn't actually been here to see him prowling the corridors like some kind of middle-aged Rambo.

Sighing heavily, he got to his feet. He glanced at his watch, trying to gauge how long it would take to ride the trail bike down to the service station at the foot of the mountain where the gunny had agreed to drive the Mustang. Perhaps he should stop off at the campground on the way to phone Sherry.

He left the room, closing the door behind him, and started down the corridor, wondering idly how the wet splotches had gotten onto the carpet.

There were more wet spots at the head of the stairs, a glistening trail of them leading down the polished wood of the steps and continuing across the lobby. He stopped to examine the trail of splashes and droplets glittering in the sunshine pouring through the French doors.

Another simple explanation presented itself: Shelly arriving at the locked front door, Sherry, wet from the shower, hurrying downstairs to let her in. . . .

Except.

The trail of water led to the huge registration desk by the wall, not the front doors.

Kelly frowned, extracting the wrinkled notepaper from his pocket and looking at it again: a note that had been crumpled up and discarded, not placed where he would be sure to find and read it.

He crouched by a small puddle of water on the stairs: not a footprint, a splash, as if someone had been carrying a sloshing container, the water sloshing out over the sides.

Hurrying down the stairs, he followed the trail to the desk, leaned over the top looking for the container.

There was a wet ring on the floor behind the desk, a perfect circle the size of a dinner plate, or a bucket. Beside it, the faint outline of a large footprint marred the polished surface, still slightly damp.

Blood trail!

The old phrase popped into his mind, a leftover from his days in Vietnam. The VC always dragged their dead and wounded away after a firefight. Sometimes you could actually catch up with them by following the bright splashes of blood on the jungle floor; at least it gave you a direction to aim for.

Dropping the rifle onto the mahogany countertop, Kelly walked to the end of the registration desk, opened the carved swinging gate that separated it from the rest of the lobby, and entered the narrow corridor between the desk and the mailboxes. He placed his foot over the print on the floor, then knelt and looked up under the counter. A trigger-shaped brass lever winked at him from beneath the wood coping. He inserted his finger and squeezed.

Nothing happened.

"Damn!"

He stood and pushed against the edge of the massive desk.

Still nothing.

Turned and pushed on the panel of mailboxes.

Nada.

Frustrated, he reached beneath the desk and squeezed the lever again. Heard a faint click. Released the lever. Click again. A spring-pressure latch! He squeezed the lever and pushed against the desk. Click. Nothing. Squeezed and pulled.

Click. The whole damned thing pivoted silently around on a hidden spindle, the ease with which it turned nearly throwing him off balance.

Narrow steps covered in faded Oriental carpet led down into a void of absolute darkness, wet splashes showing on the top steps.

Blood trail!

A thin, ululating wail, as of a tortured animal, drifting up into the lobby from below.

Kelly grabbed the rifle and started down the stairs, freezing at the realization that he had to have a light. Turning and clambering back up into the lobby, he tried to remember where they had left the flashlight they'd been using the night before. A snapshot in his mind of Sherry storming up the darkened staircase with the light.

Another scream from below. The sound of it was like an icy dagger in his soul.

Immersed in a timeless void of total darkness, Sherry heard the scream. She had ceased struggling to free her hands some time before, lulled to inactivity by the seeming hopelessness of her situation. Now the sheer horror contained in the single drawn-out note spurred her brain to a renewed frenzy of activity.

Shelly!

It had to be Shelly!

The distant wail subsided to a final gurgling sob. Fuck this. She had to get out of here somehow. Kicking out with all of her might, her enraged scream bottled up behind the gag, she hit the wall with the toes of her running shoes and felt the narrow bed she was on rock.

Kick, harder!

The bed rocked again, inching away from the wall this time.

Again!

The shock sent jolts of pain up her legs, widening the gap between bed and wall.

Fuck it! Again!

The bed slid a foot away from the wall and she tumbled face forward onto a cold slab of concrete. Lying there numb and shaking, she reached out behind her with her fingers, felt the cheap metal frame of a rollaway, the sharp angled edges cutting her.

Yes, by God!

She wriggled around on the cold floor as the far-off scream knifed through the blackness again.

Tracy's scream died away as the fat man, his gross naked belly still touching her thigh, placed a finger to his lips. He straightened and stepped back into the cold shadows beyond the light.

The hysterical girl whipped her head from

side to side, arching her back and trying to rip her arms free from the leather restraints.

She didn't know how long she had been lying there since he had stopped babbling about his mother and the bad thing and gone away, leaving her alone in the cold. She had known all along he was talking about sex, though, and she realized as soon as he had disappeared that she had made a big mistake by pretending she didn't understand.

That had been really stupid. . . . If only she wasn't so horribly cold. The cold made it hard to think.

She had thanked God he had gone away, giving her time to get her thoughts together.

During his absence she had made up her mind to let him do what he wanted, even pretending that she liked it. It wasn't as if she was a virgin or anything—she had been doing it since the summer she was fourteen—and it was clear that he was completely insane. He was probably going to rape her anyway before he killed her.

Tracy had been sure that if she cooperated she could get him to free her arms and legs; maybe even make him take her somewhere warm. After that, a sketchy plan formed in her mind: She might be able to get his gun, or hit him over the head with something . . . at the very least, she could run away and hide from him. He was grossly fat and stupid and she had won three medals in track when she was in the eighth grade. . . .

First though, she would have to get him to free her arms and legs. She would smile at him, invite him to kiss her. It shouldn't be too hard, she had decided. She knew a half dozen good-looking guys who would happily do just about anything she asked for the privilege.

Then, just moments before, the fat man had appeared naked before her, his bloated white belly quivering in the harsh light above his distended purple penis. Her resolve had crumbled as the smell of his unwashed body had swept over her. Then he had made his first clumsy attempt to climb up onto the table. He had slipped, grunting like a pig as he toppled across her lower body, the massive weight of his clammy flesh crushing her thighs and buttocks against the rough wooden table.

Tracy had started screaming then, unable to stop herself in the certain knowledge that if he actually succeeded in getting on top of her she would be smashed to a bloodied pulp beneath the hideous bulk of him.

She had realized with mind-shattering clarity as he slid off the table and put his filthy finger to his blubbery lips for silence that she would rather die than have him enter her.

Shame!

Johnny stood in the dark, watching the girl who was still writhing helplessly on the table. He backed farther away, felt Farrah's cold cheek brush against his naked butt and whirled to face her. She stared at his pitiful drooping thing, but said nothing.

He knew what she was thinking all the same: He was too fat to get up on the unfamiliar table and do the bad thing to the girl. He started to explain that the overalls caught around his ankles had kept him from climbing up on Marilyn as he had intended.

He knew, however, that she would just laugh at that.

Farrah and Liz were always laughing at him.

They were jealous.

Stooping and grabbing his overalls, he pulled them on, fastening the brass hooks over his shoulders. There would be plenty of time to teach Marilyn about the bad thing, when he was done. For now, he didn't want her to think he was mad at her. After all, she was going to be his prettiest girlfriend.

He shuffled across to the table, looping the leather apron over his head on the way.

"D-don't cry no more, M-Marilyn," he said, leaning forward to clutch the terrified girl's pale face in one massive hand. "Johnny's g-gonna f-fix you now."

She stopped struggling and looked up into the small black eyes glittering behind their circling rings of fat. Her blue lips trembled as she formed the single word. "C-C-Coldddd!"

His big head bobbed up and down in sympathy. "Y-you won't n-never be cold no more," he told her. Releasing her face and turning into the darkness, he lifted Liz's body from the wooden bench and carried her back to the table, propping her up beside him. He tilted the metal reflector so that Marilyn could see, playing the glaring light against Liz's carefully stitched and made-up face.

"S-see?" he said, proudly displaying his handiwork, "L-Liz isn't c-cold."

Reaching onto the wooden chest beside the table, he lifted the razored flaying knife and held it beside Liz's blotchy cheek. "Johnny's g-gonna f-fix you even better than Liz! So you'll n-never be c-cold or h-hungry . . . or bad no more!"

Tracy Swanson's head slowly lifted from the table. She turned to regard the leathery face gazing back at her from beneath its tangle of shining black hair. The light from the hissing lanterns cast twin reflections of her own face against the dark, glassy pupils of the dead thing's eyes. The thing he called Liz.

Mercifully, Tracy's mind snapped at that instant, transporting her in a flash to some perfect Mediterranean clime where handsome Greek sailors spread soothing lotion on her back as she basked in the warmth and comfort of a perpetually shining sun. She neither heard the long, moaning wail issuing from between her own bloodless lips nor saw the fat man replace Liz on her bench before turning back to his tool chest to lift the plastic bottle of ether which would ensure that she did nothing to spoil the delicate and bloody work he was about to begin.

Regions of Hell

SILENCE.

Kelly stood on the bottommost step of the narrow staircase beneath the registration desk. The long, tortured scream had abruptly ended moments before he had begun his second descent into the dark unknown and he cursed the precious minutes that had been wasted in his frantic rush back up to the second floor, and the ensuing search for the flashlight.

He had found it beside the bed in his room. Checking to see that it was working, he had jammed it into his belt. Then, pausing long enough to wrench half a candle from the holder on his dresser and drop it and a book of matches into a pocket, he had pounded back down to the lobby and the entrance to the subterranean secrets of the Summerland Hotel.

He peered into the gloom at the foot of the

staircase, trying to determine from which direction the screams had originated. The spill of pale light from the floor above illuminated only the dusty section of the broad corridor immediately ahead of him that extended off into pitch darkness in both directions.

Stepping out into the passage, he clicked on the flashlight. To his right, cobwebbed statuary cast giant shadows across the doorless openings of two large rooms whose contents he could not see. Farther down the corridor were the outlines of several closed doors. In the opposite direction, the corridor curved away to his left, the peeling wall blocking from view whatever lay beyond the curve.

He flashed the beam along the floor in both directions, hoping to see further evidence of the water trail he had followed through the lobby, but there was nothing. Either the excess water in the container had all sloshed out by the time its owner had reached this point or any further spillage had already dried. Kelly looked both ways again, chose a direction, and clicked the M14's safety off. Pressing himself to the nearest wall and playing the flashlight beam ahead and to the side, he began slowly advancing down the dark hallway.

As he walked, the smell of something dead grew stronger in his nostrils.

Free!

Sherry's hands popped apart. Reaching down

for her ankles, she felt for the end of the duct tape securing them and began unwinding it. The tape made a loud, ripping noise as it came loose and her eyes darted fearfully around the darkened room. A moment later, her feet were free.

Dropping the tape onto the floor in a sticky ball, she ripped the double strip from her mouth, suppressing the scream of pain as she felt the skin tearing from her face. She grabbed the edge of the creaky bed and stood, then fumbled on the mattress for the form she knew was lying there.

"Shelly, are you there?" A hoarse whisper.

Her hands touched a leg clad in denim. She ran them along the body, feeling a blouse or shirt of some soft material, the swell of a woman's breasts, soft, dry skin at the opening of a collar.

The chin, the face; a peculiar feeling of dread building within her. Her hand touched a row of tiny raised stitching just below the ear—stitching of the kind you might find on the seams of a baseball.

Not a person at all, she thought as her hands touched hair, hard glassy surfaces where the eyes should be. More like . . . a doll—a life-sized doll . . .

She frowned in the dark, remembering Coolidge's words about Johnny. "Not a half-bad taxidermist when he gets the chance," and the significance of the giant doll beneath her hands hit her like an iron fist. "Oh, Jesus," she moaned, backing away from the bed and its horrible occupant. "Sweet, merciful Jesus!" He had stuffed them, the crazy bastard: kidnapped and murdered and stuffed them. All the young girls.

Something hit her across the back of her knees and she tumbled backward onto another bed. Two more bodies shifted beneath her weight and the scream that had been building in the back of her throat erupted in a short, high-pitched shriek. Her hands touched breasts and leathery skin. Tangles of hair filled her mouth as she rolled onto her stomach, struggling to get back on her feet.

She could feel her sanity threatening to slip away.

Her groping hands found the edge of the bed at last, and she stood, flailing her arms about her head as something long and slender brushed her face.

The slender thing fell into her left hand and she realized what it was. She pulled on it, flooding the room with blinding light from a single overhead bulb.

"Huh!"

Johnny stood frozen above the naked girl.

He was sure he had heard something above the hissing of the lanterns; a brief sharp squeal that might have been a woman's voice.

His needle-tipped blooding knife was poised just above Tracy Swanson's outstretched throat. As soon as the ether had taken full effect, he had raised the end of the table on blocks so that the girl's head now hung down at a thirty-degree angle above the empty bucket, the same one he had used to fetch the hot water for the bath he had so lovingly given her earlier.

He hesitated over her, anxious to get on with the preparation before the ether wore off and the girl started struggling again.

He had not counted on having to deal with the two women from the hotel, but they had parked their car just beyond the shed where he had stored the truck, blocking his access to the secret place. He had crept up through the trees and heard them talking about calling the police to begin searching for him and knew he had no choice but to take them. He had put them out with ether. Now, however, he was not sure there was enough of the ether left to put the girl to sleep again. There were already bruises on her feet and wrists from her earlier struggles and he could not bear the thought of any further damage to her soft, fair skin. Once he punctured the large vein softly pulsing below her ear, her own heart and gravity would quickly do the work of emptying her body of blood and he could stop worrying, although the real work would just be beginning, the delicate and painstaking job of taking her out of her skin, scraping away every last trace of fat and tissue from the inside.

The jointed fiberglass mannequin he had selected and prepared to fill Marilyn's skin already lay in sections on the floor beside the tub of caustic chemicals in which he would soak her fine, smooth pelt before beginning the days-long task of stitching it onto her new body.

So much to do. It would mean neglecting the other girls. They would probably be jealous. And there were still the two women to dispose of, as well. Men would come looking for them soon, he was sure.

So much to do.

He should hurry and get this part over with. Take care of the others while Marilyn was soaking. . . .

All those thoughts ran helter-skelter through his mind, and still he hesitated, cocking his ear to the door of the cold room, listening for the alien sound to be repeated. It could just be the rats—the maze of rooms and corridors beneath the old hotel was filled with them.

Probably rats.

He listened again, imagining now that he heard footsteps in the corridor. Maybe he should go to the door of the cold room and look out, just to be sure. Better safe than sorry. That was what his mother had always said.

It would only take a minute to check, and if there was anyone approaching he would see them because they would have to have a light.

The girl moaned softly on the table.

Kelly stood stock-still in the dark.

He had been exploring a large room filled with rusting slot machines and broken gambling paraphernalia when another scream had echoed through the underground complex. Running to the open doorway and switching off the flashlight, he had tried to get a fix on it by ear.

He cursed the fact that he had not been out in the corridor itself when the scream came. He had heard the short sound through the doorway, which gave him no hint as to its origin. He was about to resume his search when he heard another sound.

A door, slowly opening on rusted hinges.

This time there was no doubt as to the direction from which the sound had come. It was off to his left, opposite from the way he had come. He clicked off his flashlight and hurried back to the glow of pale illumination marking the lobby stairway. Reaching it, he strained to see into the black void beyond.

A faint glimmer of yellow light flickered against the curving wall of the empty corridor, then went out.

Lowering the M14 to his hip in preparation for a burst of sweeping automatic fire, and with the extinguished flashlight at the ready in his other hand, Kelly slowly advanced into the darkness. As he moved, he remembered the motto of the tunnel rats he had met in Nam, highly trained specialists whose only job had been to flush enemy soldiers out of stinking underground complexes like this: "Shoot first and let God sort 'em out!"

*   *   *

Johnny bent worriedly over the unconscious girl.
She moaned again and her head flopped to one
side. He realized that she was waking up.

He looked toward the door.

He had listened for a long time to the familiar
underground sounds of his secret place, even
turning down the pressure on all but one of the
hissing lanterns. There had been the scuffling of
a rat along the corridor outside the cold room, a
few of the normal drips and creaks of settling
ground and seeping groundwater.

Nothing to worry about.

No need to waste more time going out for a look.

The three lanterns hissed loudly as he pumped
the valves up to full pressure and adjusted the
mantles for maximum brightness. Squinting into
the glare, he turned the girl's head back to its
former position, placing a fat thumb on the pulsing vein at the apex of her jaw. Her upended
position had allowed the blood to flow back to
her head, restoring the color to her lips.

She was so beautiful.

Grasping the blooding knife in his sweaty
palm, he positioned it for the puncture.

"Get your hands off of her, you filthy fucker!"

The knife clattered to the floor and Johnny
stared at the dark figure silhouetted in the open
doorway.

Sherry Mahan stepped into the room, the
Beretta that had remained concealed in her
waistband throughout the ordeal held before
her in a two-handed grip. "Put your hands over
your head and step away from the table."

The fat man stared at her, his ugly mouth hanging open in utter disbelief. It was the cop stuff he had dreamed—no, had nightmares about. But it wasn't a cop at all, just one of the women from the hotel.

"I said, move!" Sherry's voice broke. She could see two more of the Phantom's obscene creations propped against the wall behind him, and the palpable stink of death was wafting into the freezing atmosphere of the room from a low, roughly hewn tunnel to his left where something that looked like a pair of skeletal legs protruded from the shadows. She swallowed hard, fighting back the bile rising in her throat. The man was still leaning close to the girl on the table, too close to risk shooting him in the poor light.

Johnny did not move.

Nobody, but especially not this stupid woman, was going to send him to the slammer.

"Goddammit, I'm warning you!" The gun was shaking ever so slightly in her hands. She had not been prepared for this. After getting the lights on and finding Shelly bound on a sofa in the room adjoining the one in which she had been held, she had untied her hysterical friend and, with the aid of a small penlight she found on a table covered with comic books, made her way out into the dark corridor beyond the Phantom's ghastly apartment. There had been a moment of panic as the hinges on the door had creaked, then they were on their way to freedom. That was when she had noticed the thin line of white light leaking out around the edges

of the thick refrigeratorlike door on the opposite wall. Pushing Shelly up against the wall, she
moved quietly to the door, found it slightly ajar,
and peered into an old storage room cut into
the living, perpetually cold rock of the mountain, seen the monster bent over the white form
on the table. . . .

Scared!

She was scared of him.

Johnny felt his heart racing in his massive
chest and he was filled with an indescribable
feeling of power. The woman could not stop
him. Nobody could stop him. He grinned a slow,
stupid grin, picturing what he would do to this
one. First, he would do the bad thing to her.
Over and over and over, until she screamed for
mercy. Then, when he couldn't do it anymore,
he would cut off her head and mount it in the
living room, just as his daddy used to mount the
heads of the animals he killed. After that, whenever he looked at it he would remember that
they could never catch him, never in a million,
zillion years 'cause he was too smart for them.

Smart like a mountain lion is smart.

All he had to do now was wait. That was all he
ever had to do. Wait. Still smiling, Johnny slowly
straightened and raised his hands.

The lanterns hissed in the cold air.

Liz and Farrah watched in silence.

"Okay, now step away from the table."

"Sherry!"

She turned her head slightly, rolling her eyes
to look at the man standing in the doorway

behind her. The muzzle of her gun drifted away from Johnny.

It was enough.

Swiping out with his ham-sized fist, the fat man smashed the glowing lanterns to the floor. The small-caliber gun in the woman's hand exploded five times in rapid succession at the spot where he had been standing, the bright blue flashes from its muzzle filling the room with an eerie strobe light that glared back from the eyes of Liz and Farrah: five stop-action images of Johnny's hand snatching up a stubby rifle from the wooden bench between the stuffed bodies.

"Sherry, get down, get down!" Kelly screamed at her, raising the M14 to fire a burst.

"No! For Christ's sake, Chris, there's a girl in here!" she shrieked, her voice rising to a frantic pitch.

There was a quick, sudden sound of footsteps and Johnny's massive bulk bowled them both over in a bone-crushing impact that flung them to either side of the open door as though they were made of straw. Sherry's little automatic clattered onto the concrete floor, Kelly careened into the stone wall with such force the wind was knocked completely out of him.

The sound of heavy feet running receded down the long corridor.

"Goddammit!" Kelly lurched to his feet, switching on the flashlight and bolting through the door. He listened for a split second before firing a long, deafening burst after the fleeing murderer, knowing even as the bright afterimage of the muzzle flashes faded from his retinas that Johnny was safe beyond the curve of the corridor.

He turned back, heard a soft whimpering sound farther up the corridor, and raised the beam of his light to see Shelly, her slacks torn at the knee and her red hair in wild disarray, stumbling toward him.

Final Resolve

JOHNNY flew like the wind down the dark corridor. He had no need for lights, he had been wandering the underground spaces of his vast subterranean world since the day he had discovered the hidden entrance by the waterfall when he was twelve. Seventy-five steps to the staircase leading up into the old hotel, a hundred and five steps to the doorway that went into the cave; he knew every inch of the place better than the inside of his jumbled mountain cabin.

His heart was filled with joy at the discovery of his newfound powers. He had escaped from the stupid woman and her companion, just as he had known he would. They could not stop him. No one could stop him.

He slowed to duck through the short passage into the cave, leaning against the wall to listen for the sound of pursuing footsteps. He hoped the man would come after him now. It would be so easy to kill him here in the dark.

The man's name was Chris and Johnny remembered who he was, why that name had been gnawing at the back of his brain since the night on the steps of the hotel.

Chris.

That was the name Diana had kept calling out on that long-ago Christmas Eve, when he had held her down on the floor of the truck. Chris, the boy in the new Buick with her, the one she had been doing the evil thing with. He hated the man, Chris. Diana had died with his name on her lips, had never forgiven him for taking her away from Chris. That was why she was not like the others, why she said the terrible things to him.

He was going to enjoy killing Chris.

More than any of the others.

Of course, he would have to kill all of them now. First Chris, then the two women.

Then maybe they would all leave him alone to prepare Marilyn.

Johnny ducked cautiously back into the short connecting passage and peered out into the long corridor. A light flickered in the distance and he knew the man was there waiting in the gloomy shadows, preparing to come and get him. A slow smile filled his round moon face and he backed into the cave to wait. The hand-rubbed walnut of his daddy's carbine was smooth and comforting in his hand.

*   *   *

Kelly dripped hot wax onto the cracked linoleum behind one of the planters by the wall and stuck the candle to it. The flame flickered in the slight draft of the corridor, casting grotesque shadows onto the opposite wall. When he was satisfied that the candle was firmly planted, he backed away, finally getting to his feet and sprinting back to the lobby stairway.

Shelly had draped her sweater over the naked girl from the cold storage room and was leading her to the stairs with comforting reassurances. Sherry stood guard over them with the small pistol she had retrieved. Her eyes met Kelly's as the two frightened women started up the stairs together.

"Is the girl going to be okay?" he asked.

Sherry nodded. "Physically, she's mostly just cold. Psychologically . . ." She shook her head. "I don't know. She doesn't even know where she is. Right now she thinks she's about eight years old and that Shelly is her mother." She looked down the dark corridor. "What about him?"

"He's down there someplace in the dark," he replied. "I figure seeing the light from the candle will keep him from coming back this way."

"There's an entrance to a huge cave down there," she told him. "It runs all the way up to the waterfall. That's how he gets in and out."

"Can I get up there on a trail bike before he makes it out?"

"I think so, but—"

"But, hell, Sherry. If this son of a bitch gets away now, he's liable to take to the woods and we'll never find him. We can trap him right now."

She nodded, knowing he was right. "What do you want to do?"

"Not very much. I'm going to go up there and cover the entrance to his cave to be sure he doesn't get out." He handed her his pistol, which was far heavier and more accurate than her little Beretta. "You keep him pinned down on this end. As soon as Shelly pulls herself together, send her out for the police." He grinned. "You and I will keep the rat bottled up in his hole until they get here."

She looked at him in surprise. "I thought you were going to kill him."

"Not unless he makes me." He reached out and squeezed her hand. "I've decided to quit the killing business cold turkey."

"What changed your mind?"

He looked into her eyes. "For a while there I thought I'd lost you. It hurt." He shrugged. "I'd like to get the rest of my life off to a fresh start. Your way."

She leaned over and kissed him on the lips. "Thank you for that."

He raised the rifle. "I'd better go. Tell me exactly where the cave entrance is."

One On One

JOHNNY had been waiting a long time in the dark cavern. After ten minutes it had occurred to him that maybe the evil man wasn't going to come for him after all. Crawling on his hands and knees, he made his way back through the short passage and looked out into the corridor. The light he had seen before still flickered in the same place, the black shadows jumping against the ceiling making it hard to tell if anyone was really there.

He considered going to investigate but stopped himself, remembering his television shows. The man might just be waiting in the dark to shoot him. He pounded his huge fist against the stones in frustration. This wasn't the way he had pictured it in his mind.

A disturbing thought popped into his head. What if the man had decided to leave and get the cops? Then he would be stuck here and they would come in with lights and get him. He couldn't let that happen.

Scrambling backward into the cave, Johnny got to his feet and ran. Once he got outside the cops would never find him. He had half a dozen carefully prepared burrows scattered about the mountainside. Places where he could hole up for weeks at a time if he had to.

The waterfall thundered down the side of the mountain, the colors of its rainbow glowing in the late afternoon sunlight.

It had taken Kelly less than ten minutes to ride up from the hotel on the powerful dirt bike, much more quickly than the killer could have made his way out of the cave if Sherry's assessment of the time she had spent walking underground was anywhere near accurate.

He hid the bike in the underbrush near the twin pine trees at the end of the pool and strode quickly across the clearing to a stand of scrub oaks fronting the rocky wall to the right of the falls. A narrow ledge angled up into the trees five feet above ground level. Keeping his back pressed to the rocks, he sidestepped up the ledge and saw the black rectangle of the doorway hidden in the dappled shadows of the foliage.

"Well, I'll be damned!" He whispered the expletive, amazed that no one had spotted the entrance during all the searches that had been conducted in the area. Pumping a round into the M14's chamber, he stepped into the dark hole and listened. He thought he could hear the faint sound of footsteps echoing up from somewhere below a flight of rusting metal stairs.

Backing out into the open again, he dropped into the clearing and scanned the surrounding terrain with a practiced eye. A dark depression twenty feet up the rock wall on the opposite side of the pool offered a perfect position from which to cover the cave entrance, providing the advantages of both height and concealment. The spot had the added advantage of placing the lowering sun directly in the killer's eyes if he looked toward it.

Slinging the M14 across his back, Kelly skirted the edge of the pool and began to climb.

Johnny reached the foot of the metal stairs and paused to catch his breath. He had run all the way from the lower end of the cave, a long uphill climb, and the sweat was pouring from his body. Now his breath came in great heaving gasps as his overworked heart tried to catch up with the demands imposed by his massive bulk.

He flopped down on the bottom step to get his breath, grateful that the path back to the truck was downhill all the way. Once he got there it would be easy to tell if the intruders were still at the hotel. If they were, he had several options open to him. He could lie in wait beside the road and shoot them as they tried to drive out, or wait until night and creep in under cover of darkness to kill them. He grinned again, thinking how easy it would be.

His face darkened as he considered the possibility that they might already have escaped. In that case, he would simply move to one of his hideaways and hole up. He was tired and he needed to eat and sleep.

His breathing had slowed and he stood, preparing to climb the long, winding staircase that represented the last physical obstacle to his freedom.

The sniper's nest was textbook perfect.

Upon reaching the top, Kelly had discovered a shallow depression filled with soft, springy grass and hidden by the long shadows of an overhanging rock shelf. Lying prone at the edge of the depression, he had a perfect field of fire across the entire clearing. Anyone stepping from the cave entrance would be perfectly silhouetted in his sights.

He ejected the magazine from the rifle and quickly counted the rounds remaining after the frantic burst he had fired in the underground corridor.

Three.

He had forgotten the M14's rapid rate of fire—seven hundred and fifty rounds per minute. The two-second burst had nearly depleted his ammunition. He would like to have had more, but given the circumstances, three rounds should be more than enough. One well-placed shot would convince the killer to stay put in the cave.

He snapped the magazine back into place, chambered a fresh round, and settled down to wait, musing that this was the last time he would ever do anything like this.

He grimaced, thinking about the fat man and the carnage he had glimpsed in the room beneath the hotel. He wanted the man dead, wanted it badly. But he had realized that he could no longer go on setting himself up as judge, jury, and executioner. Not if he wanted a new life with Sherry.

Johnny reached the top of the stairs and leaned against the iron rail to mop his brow with his sleeve. It was cool and dark in the cave and he stood there savoring the breeze wafting up from the depths. It would still be hot outside and he wasn't looking forward to getting out in the sun. But it had to be done.

Pausing to wipe his sweaty palms on the front of his overalls, he took a firm grip on the carbine and made his way to the opening on the front of the cliff face. Squinting into the sunshine, he parted the branches of a scrub oak and looked around the empty clearing.

CRRACK!

The shot from the armor-piercing bullet exploded against the rock wall a foot above his head, peppering the rolls of fat at the back of his neck with stinging fragments of stone.

Johnny dived back into the cave, tripping and falling backward onto the stone floor. Stunned, he pulled himself to a sitting position and touched his injured neck. His hand came away bloody and he bellowed like an enraged bull.

The man!

The evil one named Chris.

Johnny scrambled to his feet and stumbled back down the spiral metal stairs, howling his murderous rage into the echoing depths of the black cave.

Perfect!

Kelly rolled onto his side with a vicious grin. The killer's glistening moon face had been framed precisely in the center of his scope for long seconds and it had taken all his self-control to not simply put a round between the bastard's beady eyes and be done with it. In the end, he had let the sights drift up to a point above the man's gleaming head and fired. The target had disappeared in a cloud of dust, howling so loudly the sound had reached Kelly's ears despite the roar of the waterfall.

He doubted that Johnny would show his face again though he worried briefly about Sherry. What if the killer should double back to the hotel? He dismissed the thought. Sherry could handle herself. Hell, she had already had the drop on the fat man when he blundered into the underground room and blew it.

Rolling back onto his stomach, he settled his sights on the cave entrance and waited.

They thought he was stupid!

Everyone always thought he was stupid.

Well, he would show them who was stupid.

Johnny stepped off the metal stairs, crossed the cave to a sloping ramp of jagged black rock, and began to climb.

The man named Chris was waiting for him out there. He had known it was him the second he'd heard the flat report of the heavy rifle. He was probably up on one of the ledges above the pool, thinking he had old fat, stupid Johnny trapped.

He'd show him who was stupid.

His hands grabbed on to a protrusion and he pulled himself up onto a broad shelf littered with bat droppings. Daylight showed ahead as he worked his way forward on his belly, pushing the old carbine before him.

Pretty soon, the evil man would see which one of them was stupid.

Kelly lay on the soft cushion of grass watching the clearing. His finger rested lightly on the trigger. There had been no activity from the cave entrance since his first and only shot several minutes before.

He wondered if Shelly had been able to pull herself together enough to go for the police. He knew she was adept at riding dirt bikes, and figured it should take her no more than fifteen or twenty minutes to ride to the end of the lake to use the phone. How long would it take the police to arrive after the call, another twenty minutes? Thirty?

He glanced at his watch, figuring he should see some sign of reinforcements in the next few minutes.

Johnny slid out onto the high ledge through the narrow cave opening and looked down. The evil man was lying in a shallow depression fifty feet below him and a couple of hundred feet to his right, his back and shoulders completely exposed below the overhanging rocks.

The fat man grinned and a thin strand of saliva dribbled onto his chin to mingle with the rivulets of sweat pouring down his face.

He had won!

Wiping the smelly bat droppings off his hands and cradling the carbine against his cheek, he lined the man's shoulders up in the carbine's simple post sights and squeezed down on the trigger.

Three shots exploded from the carbine in rapid succession.

Pain!

Kelly rolled away, blinded by dust, as the first bullet ripped into the ledge, inches from his face. The second shot hit him in the right bicep and his finger involuntarily clenched down on the M14's trigger, expending his two remaining rounds harmlessly into the air. The third shot slammed into his shoulder six inches above the first.

He screamed and threw himself back against the rocks at the rear of the depression as two more shots exploded around his feet. He snatched the M14 out of the line of fire, remembering the round in his shirt pocket. Fumbling with the rifle's stiff slide mechanism, and fighting off the shock and pain of the wounds in his arm and shoulder, he tried to load the last bullet with a blood-slick hand.

He knew that he had blown it at long last, and now he was probably going to die for it.

Ironic as all hell.

Johnny whooped gleefuly and edged farther out on his ledge for a better look. He had hit the evil man at least once. Probably killed him.

"P-pretty stupid!" He screamed it into the gathering dusk, then giggled delightedly. He would finish the man off and then go back down to the hotel to kill the women.

There weren't going to be any cops.

The edge of the man's body was just visible behind the shallow overhang of rock. If he could lean out just a few inches farther, he could kill him dead for sure.

Getting to his feet, and bracing himself against

the rocks, Johnny got a clear view of the helpless man fumbling with his rifle. He grinned and raised the carbine to his shoulder.

"Damn you, Johnny!"

He froze as the sound of Diana's voice echoed out of the narrow tunnel by his feet.

"Shut up," he screamed, teetering on the ledge in sudden panic. "Shut up! Shut up!"

"You're stupid and bad, Johnny! You'll never hit him." Diana laughed at him as he raised the carbine and tried to concentrate on shooting the evil man, the one she had done the bad thing with.

Kelly cringed on his ledge, waiting for the impact of another bullet from the fat man's gun. The killer stood on the ledge above and across from him, aiming his rifle.

The maniac had outwitted him.

His numbing fingers refused to insert the single bullet into the chamber of the M14. What was the madman waiting for? He looked up as Johnny shook his head wildly from side to side.

Then, miraculously, the bloody bullet slipped into the firing chamber of the M14. Kelly raised the muzzle and squeezed down on the trigger. The gun went off with an explosive report, the kick slamming against his useless shoulder with a blinding jolt of pain.

He saw the fat man sway on the ledge above as he lost consciousness.

* * *

"Told you, Johnny!" Diana's hateful laughter rang in his ears as a bright fountain of blood erupted though his overalls.

Johnny toppled forward, falling toward the cold, dark pool beneath the falls.

He wondered as he fell who would take care of his girls. He thought he could hear them all laughing along with Diana.

EPILOGUE

I T was well after dark by the time the mountain rescue squad located Kelly and removed him from the ledge.

They packed him down to the hotel around nine o'clock on a wire stretcher, with an IV plugged into his arm. He kept squinting and looking around, slightly confused by the bright generator-driven lights, the idling vehicles, and law-enforcement types that seemed to be filling the lawn.

"Sherry?" he croaked as a dark figure leaned over him. They moved the stretcher into the light and he found himself staring up into Blackstone's familiar face. The old man just smiled benignly.

"Chris, there are two TV crews here already and more on the way. Under the circumstances, I think it's best to disassociate yourself from Harvest."

Kelly looked up at him with a stupid grin. "You can't fire me," he slurred. "I quit!"

Blackstone smiled like an evil cherub and promptly disappeared.

He felt himself being lifted into a helicopter and blinked beneath the downdraft. When he opened his eyes again, Sherry was looking down at him.

"There you are." He smiled. "Thought I'd lost you again."

"No chance, buster!" She planted a kiss on his forehead and he felt the chopper lifting off into the cool night air.

MICHAEL O'ROURKE lives in Southern California with wife and manager, Sally Smith, and four exceptionally wise felines.